LEBANON RED

LUKE McCAFFREY

www.blackrosewriting.com

Printed in the United States of America

Black Rose Writing | Texas

ISBN: 978-1-68513-002-2
PUBLISHED BY BLACK ROSE WRITING
www.blackrosewriting.com

Printed in the United States of America
Suggested Retail Price (SRP) $18.95

Lebanon Red is printed in EB Garamond

*As a planet-friendly publisher, Black Rose Writing does its best to eliminate unnecessary waste to reduce paper usage and energy costs, while never compromising the reading experience. As a result, the final word count vs. page count may not meet common expectations.

For Georgie,
Scarlett, Savanna & Stella

LEBANON
RED

PROLOGUE

There was a steady hum. A vibration that rose through the cabin floorboards, and it was difficult to ascertain whether it was being heard or felt, or both. The window shade was cracked, and a slice of fading light cut across his lap. Outside, below the outstretched wing, a field of pink cotton clouds stretched as far as his eyes could see before succumbing to the brightness of the sun. There was a sense of security in being so high above the world, suspended between realities. Safe from all that was left behind or what was still to come. His thoughts wandered back to his final week in Idaho.

"This is the real deal, Poet," Preston Knox had said when he handed him the passport. "Commit every last bit to memory."

O'Hara opened the small booklet. Inside was a photo of himself alongside the biographical details of Donovan Burke, his new identity. He looked up at the man.

They were surrounded by heavy farm machinery with a mechanic's workshop on one side and large barrels of feed organized into rows, opposite them. O'Hara leaned against the oversized tire of a combine harvester and thumbed through the pages.

"We looked up the address. It's in Dorchester. Tough neighborhood. Totally believable a guy like you would come out of there."

"Have you never heard a Boston accent?" O'Hara asked.

"East Coast, close enough. Arabs won't know the difference. We also picked you up a few things to help you look the part." He reached into a plastic bag that had been resting on one of the barrels and removed a black ball cap and a navy blue folded shirt. When he turned the hat around O'Hara saw that the front of it contained the black and gold Boston Bruins emblem. He then tossed the shirt to O'Hara. "Bruins and Red Sox. Beantown boys are religious about their sports teams."

"So are Bronx boys," O'Hara said, without looking at the shirt and tossed it back to him. "You can keep that. I'll take the hat."

Preston chuckled. "Use tonight to work on committing all the passport details to memory and develop some backstory. Don't just know the obvious, date of birth, address, neighborhood. I want you to know the names of your relatives. Your closest friends. The high school you went to, or got kicked out of. The starting lineup for the Bo-Sox and whether or not they suck during this whole throwaway season."

O'Hara listened to the man, respectful of the fact that he was more than just a simple farmer and appreciating that when he spoke, he drew from a life of experience in such matters.

"How'd he die?" O'Hara asked, tapping the passport.

Preston shrugged. "As far as you're concerned, he didn't."

O'Hara looked back down at the passport and shook his head.

"You'll be in good hands, Poet," Preston added, as if reading his thoughts. "These guys make their American counterparts look like the JV squad."

He broke from his memories to pour another airplane bottle's worth of bourbon into his cup of ginger ale. He wondered if he would ever see Preston again, or if Idaho would be the last place he would ever see of his homeland. He stirred the drink with his finger and glanced across the aisle at the gray-haired man traveling with him. Reclined in his seat and wearing an eye mask and with headphones covering his ears, O'Hara listened to him snore, wondering how anybody could sleep at all knowing what lay ahead — while he resorted to using alcohol to flush the anxious thoughts from his own mind. He observed the man for some time, imagining what kind of life one must live to develop such an emotional and psychological threshold. He remembered their first moments alone with one another...

Pine needles covered the narrow trail so thick that, at times, they lost their footing along the rocky slope as they climbed.

"You will have to stay focused when you arrive," Yoni said without looking back. "It is a devil's playground." The man's accent was hard to place, and if O'Hara had not already known where he was from, he could easily mistake him for an Eastern European of some sort.

"How so?"

"It is an easy place to find trouble. The pandemic and failed economy have opened it up to gangsters. Terrorists. Take your pick."

"Who am I linking up with when I get there?"

"I cannot tell you much about them, but you have my word that they are the best I have. Which is why they work such an important theater." He stopped and allowed O'Hara to catch up to him. "You must understand. If anything occurs between now and then that causes you to not go, I cannot risk you having any knowledge about their identities."

"Will you be there?"

"I spent plenty of time there during the war years. But it is unlikely you will see me. If you do, something has gone wrong."

When O'Hara's mind returned to the present, the steady hum of the craft could still be heard. Outside the window, there was a break in the clouds below where he could see one of the seven seas glistening under the fading sunset. Not knowing which ocean he was looking at brought with it the realization that there was a great deal he did not know about the the world outside of his country's borders. Outside of his city, even. As his eyes grew heavy and began to close, he questioned whether his innate ability to persevere — that survival instinct that had served him well on the streets and in prison — could still be relied upon beyond those borders.

CHAPTER ONE

Beirut, Lebanon — July 2020

The moon was near full, and illuminated the subtle crests of the slow-moving black Mediterranean swells. As they shuttled toward the shrouded coastline on the military-grade, inflatable boat, O'Hara pulled the ball cap down low over his brow and stared up at the constellations above. The serenity of the cloudless night sky was entrancing, and gave him a feeling that he was being lulled into a false sense of tranquility, possibly even a trap. He had an idea of what existed beyond the beaches where they were headed, and knew what type of danger inhabited the land. He inhaled the humid ocean air and considered whether he was prepared for what lay ahead. He would soon be left to navigate alone.

The boat pilot was a nameless Israeli with short-cropped hair and a beard. The man had not spoken a word, and O'Hara was not sure he even understood English. They breached a stretch of the shoreline at a speed that caused the craft to exit the water and skid up along the pebbled beach. The boatman immediately silenced the outboard engine and hopped out. O'Hara did the same.

"You help me push," the man said, in heavily accented English. He gestured toward the boat and then the water.

O'Hara fastened the straps of his knapsack tight around his shoulders, then helped the man turn the boat around. Together they pushed it back into the water. When the man was knee deep in the ocean, he looked back at O'Hara.

"You go up stairs. Taxi." He turned and climbed aboard his craft. He pulled an oar from within and used it to paddle beyond the gentle waves that lapped at the shore. O'Hara listened to the engine kick back on. After an initial rumble, the boat sped out into the darkness.

O'Hara looked up the coastline where very few lights of the Beirut high-rises glistened among the black of night. The beach was lined with palm trees. A single cement staircase cut a path through them. He climbed the stairs to a street where he found nothing but a derelict restaurant with a torn awning. A brown Peugeot was parked along the curb. He noticed the headlights of the car flicker on and off. The engine started and the car drove alongside him, and stopped.

The driver's window lowered, revealing a man who had the face of an Arab, with dark skin, wavy black hair and a well-kept beard. "Get in," the man said in English.

O'Hara went to open the rear door, which was locked.

"The front."

O'Hara circled behind the car and climbed into the seat beside the man, who then drove down the narrow road before turning into a labyrinth of smaller alleyways.

"Welcome to Lebanon," the man said. "I am Omar."

"Donovan," O'Hara said, still getting used to the name.

"If you sit in the back seat of a taxi, they will be more likely to think you are *ajnabi*. A foreigner." Omar was wearing a loose-fitting t-shirt and khaki pants, and had thick forearms that flexed as he turned the steering wheel to navigate the Peugeot through the narrow streets. O'Hara watched him, waiting for him to say something that confirmed he was Yoni Kaplan's guy.

"You have a gun," Omar said, which sounded more like a statement than a question.

O'Hara tapped his knapsack, where it lay on his lap.

"I suggest you keep it somewhere on your body. In this country, if you ever need it, it won't be a situation where you have time to fetch it from your pack."

O'Hara unzipped his bag, removed the Glock, and tucked it at his waist.

"Where are we headed?"

"To your flat in Ras Beirut. My colleague is waiting there." Omar glanced over. "The flat is secure. We can talk freely, there."

O'Hara looked out the window. They were now driving along a tree-lined boulevard that ran parallel to the sea along the city's edge. The squat, stucco-patched structures he had first encountered had now given way to taller buildings that overlooked the moonlit ocean from their perches atop cliffs. In the distance beyond the buildings, O'Hara could make out the jagged shape of a mountain range, just a shade darker than the night sky.

As they turned off the waterfront thoroughfare and drove up the steep hills into west Beirut, the warm air that flowed through the open windows of the car brought with it scents of roasted meats and flavored tobacco smoke. There weren't many cars traveling the street, and all but a few blocks were empty of people. Those that were present were sitting on chairs along the sidewalk, smoking cigarettes or water pipes. Omar parked curbside in front of a two-story corner building, of which the ground level consisted of a commercial storefront with metal shutters pulled down over the windows. There was a metal sign over the doorway adorned with Arabic script and an image of a bread loaf.

"Your flat is above this bakery," Omar said.

O'Hara looked up at the windows. Over the entrance of the bakery was a small terrace with a glass-paned French door, through which he could see that the interior of the apartment was dimly lit.

"The best *baklava* you will ever taste is in this place."

"It'll be the only baklava I've tasted," O'Hara said.

They got out of the car and O'Hara followed Omar toward a small doorway beside the bakery. The Israeli was short in stature but with an apelike physique of broad shoulders and hands that appeared exaggerated in size. He used a key to open the door and they climbed a set of stairs up to a landing, where he knocked on a second door. Locks could be heard turning, and the door swung inward.

Standing before them was a tall, attractive woman, wearing thick-framed glasses and with auburn hair wrapped up in a loose bun above her head. She was dressed in a silk shirt and suit pants with a pair of suede house slippers on her feet. She motioned for them to enter.

"*Marhaba*," she said. "I am Layla."

"Donovan," O'Hara said.

She grinned. "You thought you would be meeting another man?" She spoke English with less of an accent than Omar.

He grinned. "It's not that."

"Don't underestimate her," Omar said. "She has the kiss of death."

"Don't listen to him," Layla said, and gestured toward two couches in the lounge room near the front door. "Get comfortable, we have much to discuss. There is wine already opened, unless you have another preference. Are you hungry?"

"No, thank you. Wine is plenty," O'Hara said.

"*Gamani*," Omar added.

The two men kicked off their shoes and sat on opposite couches, facing one another. The apartment was small and smelled of lavender, with a narrow kitchenette off the lounge room, a bathroom and a second doorway, which O'Hara assumed led to a bedroom. The large French door that opened onto the terrace was located opposite the kitchenette. The walls were bare but for an iron-framed mirror that hung near the main entrance.

O'Hara observed Layla in the kitchen where she was busy pouring red wine into long-stemmed glasses. She had the stiff-backed posture of a ballerina, long in the neck and torso, and her lower body was thick in the thighs and hips in a way that caused her pants to fit snug in those areas.

"Did you know that Lebanon produces some of the best red wine in the world?" Layla asked, as she walked back in from the kitchen carrying three filled glasses. She set them down. "I rate it second best, after Australia."

They each grabbed a glass. Omar raised his in a toast.

"*L'Chaim*," Layla said.

O'Hara nodded and sipped his wine. "This is good," he said.

"Bekaa Valley." She raised her glass. "Famous for this, and Hezbollah."

"And now Russian training camps for American anarchists," Omar added.

"Bekaa is where your friend is," Layla said.

O'Hara took another sip. Even now, months after first hearing the story, he still had trouble imagining Red being trained by Russians in the birthplace of Hezbollah.

"Donovan," Omar began. "Let's discuss the way things are going to work, here."

"Donovan is such a long name to say, every time. I'm going to call you Doni," Layla said. With her accent, she pronounced it similar to the name *Tony*.

"You can call me whatever you want."

"Doni, let's first introduce ourselves. You know where we are from and who we work for, but now erase that from your mind." Layla placed her palm on her chest. "Here, I am Layla Haddad, a twenty-six-year-old Moroccan graduate student at the American University of Beirut. I also work as a bartender at Bar Sofia, on Makdessi street."

"Bar Sofia, you will soon learn, will become the focal point of our operation," Omar added. "My name is Omar al-Awamleh. I am a thirty-five-year-old Egyptian who is living here, working as a taxi driver."

"And how is Donovan Burke..." he paused, "How am I supposed to know you guys?"

"You don't have to worry about knowing me," Omar replied. "We will mostly meet clandestinely. Taxi rides, situations like this."

Layla leaned forward and touched his hand. "You know me because, as an undergraduate, I studied abroad for a semester at Boston University. There, we became close friends, and we have kept in touch ever since."

Listening to her speak, O'Hara already believed in Layla Haddad. It was almost as though he had actually known her for as long as her narrative claimed. He would have had a hard time believing she could have gone by any other name.

"If anyone questions your friendship with Layla and tries to find you on social media, the reason they will discover nothing is because you are, how do you say it?" Omar paused and snapped his fingers. "You are into shady business. You stay off the internet because of this. After you have made your presence known at the bar and the right people begin to wonder about you, we can let it slip that you are away from Boston because maybe you have gotten into some trouble back there."

"Won't that draw attention to me in a bad way? Get people looking more closely into my story?"

"This is Beirut, *habibi*," Omar said, with a shake of his head. "Bar Sofia is owned by a man named Viktor Kuznetsov, a Russian gangster." He tapped a thick finger on the table top. "Ever since Syria, the Russians are here to stay. They run small pockets of the city."

O'Hara looked at Layla, who patted his knee with her hand.

"Your African-American friend that is being trained by Russians up in the Bekaa..." Omar waited for O'Hara to look at him before continuing, "Every few weeks they travel down to Bar Sofia to party. Alcohol, women. Viktor makes sure they are well taken care of, because of his connection to members of the Volk Group."

"I've heard a lot about this Volk Group," O'Hara said.

"They are trouble," Layla said. "They are not only operating in the Middle East, but all across Africa, as well. Elite soldiers handpicked by the Kremlin. They act as a private military outfit and do not represent the Russian state. At least not overtly. These are hard men who operate outside the law. Many of their actions in Syria and Ukraine are nothing short of war crimes. You will never manage to access their camp in the Bekaa. So, in order to meet your friend, we will have you cross paths with him inside Bar Sofia. A casual thing. I will know ahead of time when they will next visit Beirut. But it is important that you develop a presence at the bar before this occurs. You must entrench yourself there as a regular."

"You were in prison," Omar said.

O'Hara looked at him. "I was."

"Enter Bar Sofia with a similar mindset as the one with which you would have had to enter prison. Don't just be another guy drinking, easily overlooked. When you walk in, carry yourself in a way that causes the people to take notice of you."

"This is the type of place where you can just as easily broker a deal for a suitcase bomb as you can order a gin and tonic," Layla said. "I will help you navigate the crowd and know who is who."

"So I'll show up at this bar as though I am there to see you?"

She nodded. "Tomorrow evening, you will come in and see me for the first time in many years. We will make them believe our story is true." She winked.

O'Hara took a drink of wine.

"My boss, Viktor's partner in Bar Sofia, is a Lebanese man named Ali Aziz. He is a local drug dealer turned businessman. The kind of guy that can get his hands on anything you need in Beirut. Knows all the right people. His major moneymaking scheme is the production and smuggling of captagon into the Syrian battlefields."

"What's captagon?" O'Hara asked.

"They call it the warrior drug," Omar said. "Many of the militias over there stay high on it, in battle."

"Gaining Ali's attention will be your first step toward securing your place in the bar. As I said, I can help you with that. Then we can work on getting you introduced to Viktor."

Omar stood and walked over to a small table near the window. He unplugged a cell phone from a charging cable and handed it to O'Hara.

"This is yours. It is safely registered under your name, and this address. Layla's mobile number is programmed. Mine is not." He turned the phone over, to show O'Hara a series of handwritten numbers taped on the back. "This is my number. Once you have it memorized, discard the tape."

O'Hara accepted the phone and slipped it into his pocket.

"Where in Beirut do both of you live?"

"I am close to here," Layla said. "Across from the main entrance to AUB. Omar lives down south."

"Egyptian taxi drivers can't afford to live in the good neighborhoods, so I'm stuck down in the slums." Omar added.

"How's your Arabic?" Layla asked.

"Nonexistent."

"French?"

O'Hara shook his head.

"You will survive with English, but it wouldn't hurt you to learn a few words."

"Sounds like I'd be better off learning Russian," he said, half-joking.

"It would definitely help," Omar replied.

Layla finished her glass of wine and stood. "You should get some sleep. You will need to adjust to the time difference."

Omar stood and O'Hara did as well.

"These are to the front door," Layla said, handing him a set of two keys on a ring.

Omar placed a hand on O'Hara's shoulder. "Tomorrow morning, go to the bakery downstairs. Exit at nine-thirty and walk out into the street to hire a taxi. I will drive past in my car at that time, and will pick you up. We will do a tour of the area in daylight, so you can get to know the landscape."

O'Hara pulled the phone from his pocket and checked the time. He nodded.

"Then at night, you will come to the bar and see me."

Omar let go of O'Hara's shoulder. He handed him a roll of Lebanese pound notes wrapped in a rubber band. "Use this to buy yourself breakfast."

O'Hara took the money and slipped it into his pocket. He extended his hand to Omar, who clasped it. "Thank you both," he said.

Layla leaned in and kissed O'Hara on the cheeks three times, alternating sides with each kiss. "In Lebanon it's three kisses, always."

"I'm not kissing you," Omar said, and grinned.

He opened the door and stepped out onto the staircase landing. Layla followed behind. She turned around and winked, and mouthed the word *salaam*.

O'Hara shut the door behind them and turned the bolt lock above the doorknob. He pulled the Glock from his waist and set it down on the coffee table, next to the empty wine glasses. He picked them up and carried them to the kitchen sink, then found a toothbrush and toothpaste inside his knapsack. He stripped down, folded his clothes, and laid them on the coffee table, then took his gun into the bathroom and set it on a shelf above the sink. He unwrapped a bar of soap and took a steaming hot shower.

He felt disoriented, not knowing what the city looked like in the light of day. It was as if he had been sleepwalking and suddenly woke in a Lebanon bathroom — realizing he was in one of the most infamous regions of the world, involved in something so dangerous. He had yet to decide if he was even prepared for it.

He thought of Omar and Layla, and how, if he had encountered them on the street, he'd never have questioned whether they could be anything more than a bartender and a taxi driver. He remembered how Yoni had spoken so confidently of them. This allowed him to relax a little.

Over the sound of running water he thought he heard a noise outside the bathroom. He stepped out and grabbed his gun from the shelf above the sink, cracked the door open, and stopped to listen. Nothing. He peered into the living room. Empty. He turned the light switch off and crossed the room to the French door that opened to the terrace, scanning the empty street below. Nothing.

Back in the bathroom, he toweled off and checked the time on his new phone. It was three o'clock in the morning. He took the phone and gun into the bedroom, and climbed under the sheets. No longer able to fight off the exhaustion that had finally caught up, his mind began to drift. He found himself contemplating the recent months, the patterns and themes that were now evident. He didn't even know what this meant, but understood that he was starting to dream. His final memory was of his first day out of prison — of an encounter that felt like a welcome back to the old New York he once knew. In hindsight, it was a signpost indicating what life was going to be like in the months to come...

The fog was a slate gray. It mirrored the shade of the narrow cobblestone alley in the old city seaport. Storefronts were shuttered, and aside from a hooded figure — leaning with his back against the darkened windows of the corner brewery — not a soul was present. O'Hara walked in the direction of the docks and could taste the salt that rode the breeze past brackish water beneath the bridge. The smells of chargrilled meats and Italian restaurants were no longer as he'd once remembered them. If he closed his eyes he might have thought he were at a barren stretch of coastline.

A lone cloud hung low over the river, in marbled shades of darkness, like a bearer of bad news. As O'Hara reached the end of the alley, where stone transitioned to paved road, the hooded figure stepped away from the brewery wall and faced him.

The man was not wearing a mask. A faded blotch of ink was tattooed beside one of his eyes, like an off-colored birthmark. With a swift flick of his wrist he brandished an orange box cutter from the pocket of his sweatshirt and held the blade between them.

O'Hara swatted the man's hand to one side and brought an elbow hard across his brow. The man shuffle-stepped as though attempting to find his balance, and then dropped to one knee. O'Hara pushed the man over, striking him in the head with heavy fists, listening to the echoless thuds — five, six. Before long the man went limp. O'Hara crouched and turned out his pockets. A bus ticket. Gate money. He knew the man had recently been released. Just like himself.

CHAPTER TWO

It felt like no time had passed before O'Hara was startled awake by the haunting and hypnotic voice of a *muezzin*, who sang the *fajr azan* from somewhere nearby, calling all faithful Muslims to prayer, assuring them that God is great, and that prayer is better than sleep. He climbed out from under his bedsheet and found a pair of boxer shorts in his knapsack. He slipped them on and walked across the room and opened the window. The sky was still dark, and the streets below were empty, aside from the occasional local making his or her way to the mosque.

O'Hara closed his eyes and listened to the beautiful rendition, unable to understand the words, but feeling their magic deep in his soul. He used the moment to imprint on the universe an overwhelming feeling of gratitude for having made it into the country safely.

He leaned against the sill and waited for the azan to finish. When it did, the steady rumble of nearby generators could be heard echoing in all directions. Lights now shone against the sidewalk through the bakery windows below, and the sounds of pots and pans clattering and oven doors being shut indicated that the workday had begun. Rich smells of brewed coffee and fresh baked bread now filled his room as he lay back down on the bed, feeling an inexplicable sense of tranquility. He closed his eyes.

When he awoke for the second time, hours had passed. He showered and dressed in a new pair of jeans and a white t-shirt. Slipping the phone in his pocket, he tucked the Glock at the small of his back. He pulled on a button-down shirt, leaving it untucked to cover the gun. He locked up the apartment and walked downstairs to the bakery. There was an open serving window where a man was leaning out watching people in the street. He was elderly with dark, craggy skin and gray hair, and was wearing a paper mask pulled down to his chin. When O'Hara stopped in front of him, the man pulled the mask up over his mouth and nose.

"*Marhaba*," he said.

"Good morning," O'Hara replied.

"Oh, new man upstairs," the man said in English, and pointed toward the ceiling.

O'Hara smiled and nodded.

"You come inside," the man said. He called out in rapid Arabic over his shoulder and walked toward the front door, which he unlocked and opened. He beckoned for O'Hara to enter.

O'Hara pulled a cloth mask from his pocket and slipped the loops around his ears. Once he was inside, the man locked the door.

"I am Anwar," he said with a heavy accent, placing his palm against his chest.

An older, portly woman shuffled out from the kitchen, smiling. She was wearing a purple *hijab* wrapped around her head, and a matching colored *abaya* gown, and her hands were covered in white cooking flour.

"My wife, Mona," Anwar added, before saying something to her in Arabic and touching his mask.

The woman stopped and turned back toward where she had come from, but O'Hara picked up on the meaning of what had been said and held his hand up.

"You don't have to wear it for me," he said, and pulled the mask from his face.

Mona smiled and looked at her husband, who removed his mask as well.

"You never know who will cause problems about masks," Mona said in English.

"You speak English?" O'Hara asked.

"Yes, I learned many years ago in school. Anwar understands, but does not speak with confidence."

O'Hara looked at Anwar. "You speak English well."

Anwar grinned widely. "American?" he asked.

O'Hara nodded.

"We love foreigners," the man replied.

Anwar spoke to Mona in Arabic and then looked at O'Hara. "Coffee, yes?"

"Yes, please." He looked at Mona. "And I hear you have the best baklava?"

They both smiled at this.

"Yes, yes," Anwar answered as he walked behind the serving counter. "Baklava. Fresh."

"Please sit," Mona said and motioned toward a table with chairs.

O'Hara sat down and waited as the couple fumbled around behind the counter. Mona carried over a tray of golden pastries, glazed with honey and stuffed with ground pistachios. She set the tray down. "Baklava," she said, and sat on an empty chair.

"Thank you very much," O'Hara said, and touched his chest.

Anwar stepped out from behind the counter carrying a plate, balancing three small cups of coffee. He set each one down and then sat.

"Turkish coffee. You know this?" he asked.

O'Hara lifted his cup and sipped the strong, gritty brew, unable to remember the last time he had felt such a desire for caffeine. Mona used a knife to cut him a square of baklava. As he ate the pastry he closed his eyes and relished its sweet honey taste, then washed it down with more coffee. "Delicious," he said. "Thank you."

Anwar and Mona smiled and looked at one another. Mona motioned for O'Hara to take another piece, which he did.

"Where do you live in the states?"

"Boston," he lied.

"What is your work?" Anwar asked.

"I was an ironworker." O'Hara whistled and pointed upward. "Building tall buildings."

"Builder," the man responded with a nod. He said something to Mona in Arabic.

"He wants me to tell you that when he was a youth, before becoming a baker, he built with bricks."

"Bricklayer," O'Hara said.

Anwar nodded. "I do this."

"Well, I feel very lucky to have you both as my neighbors," O'Hara said, finishing the small amount of coffee. "It has been a pleasure to meet you."

"Yes, *habibi*, it is our pleasure as well, *ilhamdulillah*," Mona said.

O'Hara glanced at the screen of his cellphone. "I must get going now, but how much do I owe you for the wonderful coffee and pastries?"

Anwar clucked his tongue and wagged a powdered finger. "We are friends."

"You do not pay today, when we first meet," Mona said.

O'Hara gave a conceding shrug and stood, touching his chest. He fished a ten-thousand pound note from his pocket and left it on the table. "Gratuity," he said.

Anwar looked at his wife with a confused look, at which she explained something in Arabic. Anwar then touched his chest and bowed his head.

"Thank you very much," he said to O'Hara.

"You both have a great day," O'Hara replied.

"*Insha'allah*," they each said.

O'Hara glanced at his phone, timing it so that he exited the bakery at exactly nine-thirty. As he stepped off the sidewalk onto the street and raised his arm in the air, Omar's brown Peugeot pulled up alongside him and stopped. O'Hara opened the passenger door and climbed in.

Omar was wearing sunglasses and a nylon button-down shirt and smelled of strong cologne. Brown prayer beads hung from his rearview mirror. "*Ahlan, ya habibi*. Did you try the baklava?"

"You weren't kidding," O'Hara replied. "That was good stuff."

Omar drove the taxi down a series of narrow side streets before turning onto a wider avenue headed east which was lined with cafes, restaurants and commercial businesses. Most of the restaurants appeared closed and only a handful of people sat at the outdoor tables in front of the cafes.

"This is Hamra street. The main avenue in the area." Omar pointed a finger at rubble and trash strewn along the curb. "This mess is from riots."

"Who's rioting?"

"Everyone. They are fed up. The Lebanese pound is worthless."

"No shit, I just tipped a guy ten grand."

Omar nodded. "Also, the pandemic has made them feel like caged animals in their homes, in which they can't even keep the lights on. Nowhere to go. Nothing to do. They don't trust the government."

"Sounds like everywhere else in the world."

"You would think the riots occurred last night, but that is not the case. Beirut is bad about collecting its trash."

"Why's that?"

Omar shrugged. "Politics and poor leadership. Their energy sector is a mess, as well. You will see entire sections of the city lose power for hours." He turned off Hamra street at a corner where four uniformed officers were standing guard, lazily smoking cigarettes with machine guns slung over their shoulders.

"What's with the soldiers?" O'Hara asked.

"They are for show. If Hezbollah or any other group came here and started shooting in the streets, you would see these toy soldiers flee."

They drove down a hill where, in between buildings, O'Hara could see the turquoise waters of the Mediterranean sea. They turned onto another two-lane street that ran between a series of eateries to one side, and the iron fence of a university campus on the other.

"This is the American University of Beirut. A very prestigious school," Omar said.

They stopped at a red light at an intersection near the main gated entrance to the university. Reaching up into the cloudless blue sky was a flat-topped tower made of tan brick, with a large clock adorning its southern face.

"On our left. That building across the street," Omar said, and gestured toward what looked like a hotel. "This is where Layla lives. That is her balcony there, on the top floor."

"Some view she must have," O'Hara said.

"It is a perk of living as a socialite instead of a taxi driver," Omar said in a facetious tone.

"Maybe if you were born prettier, you'd have gotten a better cover job," O'Hara replied.

Omar looked at him. A smile broke on his face and he sighed. "I think you and I will get along." The traffic light turned green and he continued driving.

Beyond the university, they made their way down curving hill roads lined with apartment buildings and then west alongside the *corniche*, which was what Omar called the oceanfront promenade where locals gathered under the shade of palm trees. O'Hara stared out at the stark line of the horizon, noticing the silhouette of a barge in the distance. He pondered how his own arrival in the country from somewhere out there already felt more like a story he'd been told by someone else than one from his own memory. He appreciated the beauty of the sea and thought that if he were to only look in that direction, and not at the city to his left, the setting might resemble a postcard photograph of a Greek island, or some other welcoming paradise that people often flocked to on vacation.

They traveled beside the corniche up an incline and along an overlook, where Omar then pulled the car over and parked curbside.

"You will come to learn that despite appearing to live a chaotic and busy lifestyle, Arabs spend lots of time in cafes, drinking coffee and smoking." He pulled up on the manual emergency break. "Let's go behave like Arabs."

They donned paper masks and walked over to a small cliffside cafe with outdoor seating. They took a table alongside a thick glass barrier that bordered the rocky edge. Below, set in the middle of an inlet, were two large limestone structures that rose hundreds of feet high out of the sea, as if guarding the coast like stoic sentries. There was a naturally formed tunnel at the base of one of the rocks that allowed the ocean water to pass through.

"They call those Pigeon Rocks," Omar said, when he noticed O'Hara staring at them.

A masked waiter approached their table and stood in silence.

"Coffee or tea?" Omar asked O'Hara.

"Coffee."

Omar held up two fingers and spoke to the man in Arabic. He looked at O'Hara. "Do you have a tobacco flavor you like?"

"Whatever you like," O'Hara replied.

Omar said something more in Arabic and the man nodded and walked away.

"We have a lot to discuss, but first I need to make something clear." Omar was looking out toward the sea when he said this. He then leaned in over the table and looked at O'Hara. "What is happening in the Bekaa between the Volk Group and your friend's militia, is very serious and must be compromised. But my people do not share many of the same views with your people, beyond that."

"My people?"

"Idaho."

O'Hara shook his head. "They may have sent me here, but they're not my people."

Omar did not reply.

"And let's not forget, I met your boss in Idaho."

Omar nodded. "Yoni was there, manipulating. Our hands are tied in how to handle American citizens that are threats to our country. Trust me, if the militia consisted of Africans from Africa you wouldn't be here."

Omar paused as the waiter arrived with a tray of drinks. The man placed two glass mugs of Turkish coffee in front of them and said something in Arabic, to which Omar nodded. Once the man walked away, Omar looked at O'Hara.

"The whole right-wing American, conspiracy-fearing subculture... it exists in a bubble. The rest of us are out here working to stop real threats to our existence, from real enemies. The most dangerous threat your country faces at the moment is yourselves. What I would give to have Mexico as our neighbor." He let out a snort and shook his head. "Your people are out of touch with the larger world and what is occurring within it."

"Like I said, the Idaho crew aren't my people." O'Hara picked up his coffee and sipped it. "And if we are going to be honest with one another, I also think they're full of shit."

O'Hara thought he noticed a slight grin appear on Omar's face.

"You know where I was spending my days, up until recently. They are the ones who got me out. If I turned down their request to come out here, they could have easily had me locked back up." O'Hara rested the glass on the table. "While I'm in Lebanon, you and Layla are my people."

Omar nodded. "It is good to hear you speak like this."

The waiter returned, carrying a large water pipe with two hoses attached, which he held in his other hand. He placed the water pipe on the floor beside them and rested the hoses on the tabletop. The mouthpieces at the end of the hoses each had plastic disposable covers slipped over them.

"*Shukran*," Omar said to the man, who walked away. He picked up one hose and gestured toward the other. "Yoni likes you, though. Despite his feelings about the rest of them."

O'Hara picked up the other hose.

Omar pulled on his mouthpiece. The sound of bubbling water could be heard from within the wide base of the pipe. "He said they called you Poet." Clouds of smoke slipped from his mouth with his words.

O'Hara nodded.

"Are you a writer?"

O'Hara shook his head.

"Then why?"

"You know how nicknames are," O'Hara said.

Omar glanced over his shoulder and repositioned himself in his chair. "Smoke," he said. "It is lemon flavored."

O'Hara pulled on the mouthpiece, causing the pipe to bubble more, and inhaled the cool smoke. He closed his eyes and held it for a moment before exhaling, feeling his stomach muscles relax.

"You ever smoke *nargila*?" Omar asked. "We call it *sheesha* back in Cairo." He winked and took another drag from the hose.

"Nope," O'Hara replied.

"The apple flavor is very popular, but I prefer this." Omar studied him as he smoked. "Tell me about your gangster friend, Ingleton."

O'Hara sipped his coffee. "He's no gangster."

Omar released a ring of smoke from his lips.

"At least he wasn't when I last saw him," O'Hara added.

"When was that?"

"Four years ago. Before I went to prison."

"What was he, if not a gangster?"

"He dabbled in side hustles. Small jobs, really."

"Jobs?"

O'Hara did not answer him for a moment. He leaned back in his chair. "Robbing drug dealers. Burglaries. Things like that."

"You used to do these things?"

"I've done them."

"And he did them with you?"

"Come on, Omar. With who you work for, surely you know all about Red."

Omar grinned. "I didn't know you called him Red."

O'Hara nodded. "Jared. Red."

"Well, Red should have known that it's never a good idea to get involved with Russians."

O'Hara nodded. "Do you have any clue how he was recruited? How he got over here?"

"It seems each of the members were carefully selected, and recruited by Russian intelligence in the States. They came over in small groups of two and three, and reunited in the Bekaa. Some of them flew into Turkey, others into Jordan. Then they were snuck across the borders into Lebanon. This kind of thing has become much easier with the chaos next door."

"Is it true that they plan to carry out an attack on a Jewish settlement in the Golan?"

Omar hovered his hand over the table, suggesting that O'Hara lower his voice.

"We believe that is likely. But the Volk Group runs a very secure operation, up there."

"And I'm expected to eventually gain access to this training camp?" O'Hara asked.

Omar clucked his tongue. "For now, we just expect you to make the connection with your friend Red when they next come to Beirut for alcohol and women. After that, we will determine the next step."

"That sounds like a more realistic game plan than what they were saying in Idaho."

Omar batted a hand at the air. "*Habibi,* those men are role-playing. You are now among professionals."

O'Hara smiled and took a drag from the water pipe. Down below, there were two men in a speedboat rounding Pigeon Rocks.

"We will have to be careful about being seen together in public after today." Omar finished his coffee and rested the empty glass on the table. "Once you've been to Bar Sofia, I suspect people will start watching you, and looking into your background."

"Russians?"

Omar nodded. "And eventually others. Hezbollah. Iran, maybe."

"Jesus," O'Hara said, and drank the last of his coffee.

"Maybe Jesus, too," Omar replied with a grin.

"So I should assume I'm always under surveillance."

"It would be the safest way to operate." Omar tapped a finger on the table. "You must understand, you washed up on the shores of spy city. With a war right next door, and Israel to the south, everybody has representation here. I imagine that if you stay long enough you will even have your own country looking into you."

"Are they compromised?"

"Who?"

"American intelligence."

Omar shook his head. "It depends who you ask, right?"

"I'm asking you."

Omar picked up his nargila hose and puffed on it, looking at O'Hara through the smoke he exhaled. "If I were in Idaho, I would say yes. But if I were someone that held opposing views, I'd probably say they were glue holding your country together, right now."

"Which are you?"

"I am neither." Omar exhaled two streams of smoke through his nostrils. "You know what I am."

"An Egyptian taxi driver," O'Hara said.

"That is correct." Omar grinned. He pulled a wallet from his pocket and fished a few large notes from within. He laid them on the tabletop beside the empty glasses. "I will drive you past Bar Sofia, so that you know its location. It is walking distance from your flat."

He stood, and O'Hara did as well. They walked back to the Peugeot. Once inside the car Omar retraced the route they had traveled, down the steep curve along the corniche and up past the university clock tower where he then turned onto Makdessi street. As they drove past the bar, Omar gestured a thumb in its direction, without looking at it himself.

"There she is," he said.

The red brick exterior of the bar contained only one window and a black door, with an overhead sign that read Bar Sofia in black, English lettering with red Arabic script running beneath the name.

"Is it open?"

"I do not know, but there are probably people inside."

They continued on down the street, where Omar pulled over curbside and had O'Hara wait in the car while he bought them two chicken kebab, pita bread sandwiches from a vendor on a footpath between Makdessi and Hamra streets. He then drove to O'Hara's flat and parked the car out of sight from the bakery windows. He reached in his pocket and pulled out a folded envelope.

"This was passed on to us from your Idaho friends. Mixed American and Lebanese bills." Omar handed O'Hara the envelope. "But I would not carry all that around at once. Many people in this city are poor and hungry. You don't want anyone knowing you have money."

"Thanks," O'Hara said and slipped the envelope into his pocket. "Where did the money come from that you gave me last night?"

"That was from me."

"Here, let me return that," O'Hara said, reaching into his pocket.

Omar clucked his tongue. "*Wallihemak*, Lebanese pounds are practically worthless these days. You keep it."

"Well, thank you," O'Hara said.

Omar nodded. "*Yalla*," he said, and gestured for O'Hara to get out of the car.

As he walked toward his building, O'Hara could feel the bulk of the envelope pressing against his thigh. He had not opened it but could tell from its size and weight that there were many bills inside. He entered the front door and climbed the stairs, thinking of the men from whom the money originated.

CHAPTER THREE

Idaho — June 2020

They had been driving in silence for some time, O'Hara appreciating the beauty of the land through the open windows. The mountain peaks beyond gorges and deep canyons, pointed up toward the sky in a collage of highlighted browns and greens, speckled with cloud shadows. O'Hara imagined that the scene contained the same uncorrupted beauty that westward exploring pioneers would have encountered hundreds of years earlier.

"I've got some things to confess," Preston said, breaking the silence. "And what I'm about to lay on you is only known by a handful of people, so you don't need to worry." He paused to give O'Hara the chance to respond, before continuing. "I know what you went to prison for. Stealing them jewels."

O'Hara glanced at the pistol at Preston's waist.

"I also know why you were released early." Preston looked over at him. "Did you ever wonder why you were the only young and healthy inmate who got out on account of the virus?"

"I didn't give a shit."

"Well they were all old or sick. Your Albanian cellmate didn't make it out. He was in that high-risk category. If he catches the bug, it could be the end of him. Wouldn't it have made more sense to free a guy like him than you?"

"What are you saying?"

"I'm saying it wasn't the bat-eater disease that got you sprung early." Preston squeezed the steering wheel tight and grinned. "I'm saying you're not in Idaho by accident." He gestured toward the windshield. This community you're in now has a long reach."

"I'm here for the money I was offered. To come and put down roots."

"Yeah, incentives." Preston let out a snort of air. "There ain't no such thing as a free lunch, friend."

Preston guided the Land Rover up a slope and over a ridge where they picked up a pack trail that lead them back toward the canyon.

"There's some guests waiting for us, back at the bunker. Let's head on over and you'll see the bigger picture why you're here."

* * *

The four men gathered around a long wooden table in the parlor room of Preston's underground bunker. There was a crystal decanter of brandy set out among four glasses, each filled with the dark liquor.

The senator cleared his throat and spread his palms out on the table top, taking a minute to gather his thoughts. His strong jaw and full head of dark hair made it difficult to guess his age but O'Hara figured him to be significantly younger than Preston and Yoni Kaplan, who were seated beside him.

"First off, Mr. Poit, allow me to thank you for coming all the way out west." He offered a disarming smile that revealed a row of white, capped teeth before continuing what was clearly a rehearsed monologue. "I wanted to meet with you because," he paused for a moment, "well, the sad truth is that our country is in trouble. You look out there at any of these American cities. Minneapolis, Seattle, Denver, your own New York. Utter pandemonium in the streets. Defund the police and all that nonsense. But do not be fooled. What appears to the naked eye as chaos and riots has actually been an organized effort all along, backed and funded by a global elite who lurks in the shadows and pulls the puppet strings. The Antifas and the BLMs are just pieces being manipulated across the chessboard. The media outlets, with their disinformation and false reporting on the pandemic, and racism, are all controlled by these same puppet masters whose goal is to undermine the president, sterilize the police, and abolish law and order in our cities. Presenting it as though it all unfolded organically. I'm sure an intelligent man like yourself must have questioned the coincidental timing of this whole pandemic?"

O'Hara sipped from his glass of brandy.

"Election year. A bit convenient all this starts happening, no?"

"With all due respect, Senator," O'Hara said. "I follow what you're saying. But I'm still waiting to understand how it has anything to do with me."

The senator nodded.

"We are witnessing the beginning of a coup, my friend, on a scale that is unprecedented. There are obvious players who have always been hell-bent on seeing us fail as a nation. The Chinas. The Russias. The Irans. But we are now facing a threat that is entrenched deeply within our very own government structure. In the intelligence agencies. In congress." He winced. "Potentially even in the White House."

The senator paused, to allow O'Hara to process all that had been said.

"And now you're telling all this to an ex-con from the Bronx," O'Hara said in a skeptical tone.

"Have you ever heard of the Volk Group?" the senator asked.

O'Hara shook his head.

"Russian mercenaries," Preston interjected. "They claim no attachment to the country's military and act independently of it."

O'Hara looked at Yoni who had so far remained silent.

"The Volk Group is run by a man named Oleg Anakovich," the senator said. "An ex-KGB and FSB killer, who happens to be one of Putin's best friends going back to their days in Dresden, together."

"Okay, I think I see where this is going," O'Hara said, facetiously, as he picked up his glass of brandy. "Is this about the time I hopped the back fence of the Russian embassy in Riverdale? I was just a kid, man."

Yoni grinned.

"Poet, be serious and hear all that the senator has to say," Preston said.

"As much as I'd love to hear that story, the answer is no. The Volk Group has flown several African-American gang members and anarchists to the Middle East and are providing them with military training in the Bekaa Valley of Lebanon, with intentions of returning them to America to infiltrate our cities and wage war on the police." The senator pointed at Yoni. "Mister Kaplan believes that some of these militants will likely also carry out attacks on Jewish settlements along the edge of the Golan Heights as a part of their training, prior to heading back here to America. Possibly as a show of solidarity with Hezbollah, at whose invitation the Volk Group is out there operating."

O'Hara glanced over at Yoni, who nodded. He then turned his attention back to the Senator. "I'm not black. I'm not Russian. I'm not a Jew. Why am I here?"

Preston slid a manila envelope across the table in front of O'Hara.

O'Hara opened the folder. Inside, was a large glossy photograph of a muscular black man, whom he immediately recognized. He felt goose bumps crawl up the skin of his arms as he studied the picture. It showed the man dressed in a tight t-shirt, tactical pants and combat boots, walking in front of a rocky backdrop. He was speaking into a walkie-talkie and had an assault rifle slung over one shoulder.

"I believe you know Jared Ingleton," Preston said.

O'Hara looked at him and then back at the photograph.

"Alright, what's the deal?" O'Hara asked. "Bringing me out here and talking in circles. Now you're showing me a picture of some black dude? Accusing me of knowing the guy?" He knew his words were wasted once he had spoken them and could sense that he was about to learn the answers to questions that had been haunting him for the last four years.

"Ingleton is a major player in one of these militant outfits that is being trained by Volk Group mercenaries."

O'Hara slid the photograph back to Preston without speaking a word.

"He is also the reason you were locked up back in New York," the senator added.

O'Hara looked at the senator.

The senator reached into the inner pocket of his tweed jacket and removed a folded piece of paper. "This is a copy of a classified document. You cannot keep it, but feel free to have a look. It is straight from the bureau, thanks to a like-minded patriot we still have there."

He handed the paper to O'Hara, who unfolded it. It was a typed document, with all the seals and crests of the Federal Bureau of Investigation. As O'Hara read it, he felt a chill settle in his chest. The document stated that Jared Ingleton had worked with the United States government in 2016 in exchange for immunity from charges he had been facing after being caught in a sting operation involving the illegal distribution of steroids and opioids.

O'Hara studied the details of the document, hoping to find an inaccuracy that might prove it a forgery. He could sense that he was being observed as he read. All three men were watching for the slightest gesture that might be interpreted as validation. The dates made sense. Even the types of steroids were accurate as to what he remembered Red having dealt. His mind began to process what it would mean if his friend had been cooperating with the government back then, before they even committed the crime that resulted in him landing behind bars.

"You're trying to tell me he was cooperating with the feds before I was even arrested?"

"I'm not trying to tell you anything." The senator gestured to the document. "It's printed right there before you." He nodded at Preston.

"This is why you've been drawn out here to Idaho, Poet," Preston said. "We believe that if we plant you in Lebanon with a credible backstory of your own, and create a scenario where the two of you cross paths, there is a good chance you can rekindle a relationship with Ingleton."

"You want me to go to Lebanon?" O'Hara laughed. "Get fucked." He finished off his brandy and poured himself another.

"Please keep in mind that Senator Tade's connections are the reason you're a free man," Preston said. "You can just as easily go back to prison, instead. You're officially in violation of your parole at this point."

O'Hara shot Preston a cold stare.

The senator cleared his throat. "We are well aware Ingleton's grandmother took you in and raised you once your parents were no longer in the picture. What were you, thirteen? Fourteen?"

O'Hara did not respond. He felt a tinge of sadness, possibly guilt, at the mention of Nan. He picked up his glass and sipped to hide his dismay.

"I believe," Preston continued, "that despite all the rhetoric that Ingleton's organization so often vomits, when the two of you cross paths he will be so overcome with nostalgia and guilt for what happened to you, that he will have no choice but to second-guess everything he's been doing out there." He laid a finger on the photo of Red. "Let's not forget, this man helped send you to prison for what should have been a long time, in order to save his own skin. You lost almost half a decade of your life over it. It would have been longer without our intervention. Nobody will understand and appreciate that concept more than him."

"Don't you have professionals that do the kind of shit you're asking me to do?"

"Except for a handful of individual patriots we must assume that all the three-letter agencies are compromised by the Deep State," the senator said.

"Get outta here," O'Hara replied with a tone of disbelief.

"That's no fake news."

"What about this guy?" O'Hara asked, and looked at Yoni. "Lebanon is in his backyard. Why don't his people handle it?"

"In this current political climate, if word got out that Israel killed African-Americans in Lebanon..." he trailed off. "Well, you're smart enough to understand why that wouldn't go over too well."

The senator looked at Yoni. "Am I right?"

Yoni nodded. "If there is an immediate threat to Israel, we neutralize it. But I can assure you that you can prevent far more damage by recruiting a single source, than by how many people you can kill."

"Then go recruit a source," O'Hara said to him.

The senator looked as though he was about to respond when Yoni held up his hand.

"I say this to you as an Israeli who does not share the same motivations as the others in this room. The reason you are having trouble believing that you are the right man for this task is because you are unaware of how dangerous..." He paused and pressed his finger to his temple, "and how brain washed these militants are. As you have been told, your friend's group is being trained by elite soldiers in the Bekaa Valley. They are there at the invitation of Hezbollah terrorists. This means Iranian influence as well." He tapped his finger on the tabletop. "I have been briefed on your history with Ingleton, and from my life of experience in this line of work, I agree with the senator and Preston. You were basically brothers in all ways but by blood. It will take something like this personal bond you share with him to alter his perception of things. Even that may not be enough. But, from the intelligence we have gathered, these men cannot be bought or persuaded through typical means of manipulation or coercion."

"Poet," the senator said, using his nickname for the first time. He waited for O'Hara to look up at him, before continuing. "If Ingleton's crew makes it back to the streets of this country, there's trouble ahead. They will commit acts of terror that cause America to tear apart at the seams. Look at how they've brought our whole system to a halt, already. And that's with a bunch of undisciplined anarchists. Now, imagine if it were trained soldiers? Forged by a mercenary outfit as dangerous as the Volk Group?"

O'Hara turned his attention back to Yoni. "And if I go out there and fail?"

"Then we will be forced to find other ways to make sure they are unsuccessful," the Israeli answered.

CHAPTER FOUR

The constant rattling of nearby generators echoed off the low-rise apartment buildings that sandwiched the narrow street. Beirut was experiencing a long stretch of daily blackouts and those locals with the means to do so were using secondary sources to keep their televisions on and their refrigerators cold. O'Hara turned the corner onto Makdessi street and made his way toward the brick exterior of Bar Sofia, where a tall, musclebound Arab bouncer was standing outside the front door with his arms folded and flexed.

"At ease," O'Hara said, as he walked up.

"*Shoo?*" the man asked.

"I don't speak Arabic," O'Hara replied.

"Who do you know here?" the man asked in English.

"Layla," O'Hara said.

The man held up a finger and pulled the door open enough to stick his head inside where he shouted something in Arabic. He stepped aside, pulling the door fully open. "*Yalla,*" he commanded.

O'Hara stepped through the doorway into a dimly lit room that smelled of clove cigarettes. The walls and ceiling were painted black and the floor was polished cement. A bar ran the length of one wall, where a half dozen men sat spread out across twice that many stools. Layla was standing behind the bar, filling a pint glass with beer from a tap. She was wearing a white tank top and her hair was tied back in a French braid. A progressive house remix of Nina Simone's 'Sinnerman' was playing from the speakers in each corner of the room.

The rest of the space was filled with scattered tables throughout, at which sat a more balanced ratio of men to women than O'Hara expected to find in a Middle Eastern bar. Bottles of uncorked wine, pints of beer, and plates of red grapes adorned some tabletops and the crowd was an eclectic mix of ages and styles. There were fashionable university-aged women dressed in form-fitting, night club attire as well as intellectual types in corduroy jackets and fedoras who would have fit better at an open-mic poetry reading than a gangster hang out. Nobody that O'Hara laid eyes on appeared to be the types of dangerous people that Omar and Layla had described the night before.

" *Ya salaam!*" he heard Layla shout out from behind the bar. He looked over to see her smiling with her hands over her mouth in a state of mock surprise. She walked out from behind the bar and embraced him with a tight hug.

"Layla," he said.

"It is so good to see you," she said with exaggerated enthusiasm. O'Hara could feel the eyes in the room focused on them. As they hugged, he noticed beyond her shoulder, a dark recessed corner of the bar where a group of men were sitting around a large table, on a raised platform.

Layla smiled and draped her arm over O'Hara's shoulder. "I am so happy you finally made it to Beirut!"

"It's good to be here," O'Hara replied.

In his peripheral vision he noticed a man walking in their direction from the dark corner. When he glanced over, a handsome Arab man dressed in a black shirt and matching pants stepped into the light. He was clean-shaven with styled hair and the top few buttons of his shirt were left undone, exposing the hairs of his chest.

"Ali," Layla said, as the man reached them. "This is my good friend, Donovan, who is visiting from Boston." She then looked at O'Hara. "This is my boss, Ali."

Ali did not smile.

"Great place you've got here," O'Hara said.

"Thank you." Ali extended his hand, which O'Hara clasped. "Donovan, did she say?"

O'Hara nodded.

"Welcome." Ali turned to Layla. "Your guest's first drink will be on me." He looked at O'Hara.

"I appreciate that," O'Hara said.

"I remember what Doni likes to drink," Layla said. She walked behind the bar and pulled a bottle of red wine down from a shelf on the wall.

"I am fond of Layla," Ali said. "How is it exactly that you two know each other?"

"We met at a bar."

Layla held out a glass of wine, which O'Hara accepted.

He nodded toward Ali. "Thanks again."

"You know me, Ali," Layla said. "I always befriend the rough guys."

"So Donovan is a rough guy?" Ali said with a slight laugh. "Beirut is filled with men like this."

O'Hara sipped his wine, thinking of how he would have already dropped the guy if he had met him in a prison yard or on the streets of the five boroughs. Real recognized real, and there was a front about Ali that he wasn't buying.

"I will return to my table." Ali gestured over his shoulder. "Welcome to Beirut, Donovan from Boston."

O'Hara raised his wine, in a gesture of gratitude.

As Ali turned away and walked back toward his corner, another woman entered the room through a swinging door at the back. She was holding a bottle of wine and a plate of grapes, and was dressed in a black tank top. Her sandy-blonde hair fell to her shoulders in a tousled, unkempt way and was a shade lighter than the honey colored skin of her face. She wore faded jeans that fit loosely around her waist, save for the way her hips filled them out.

O'Hara watched her cross the room, moving as if she were slow dancing to a tune nobody else could hear. She set the grapes and wine on an empty table where a lone man sat. The man said something that caused her to laugh. He was a pretty man with gelled hair and chiseled features, dressed expensively, with a gold chain hanging above the v-neck cut of his shirt.

"Are you even able to look away from her?" Layla asked, jokingly.

"You sound jealous," O'Hara replied.

She clucked her tongue and shook her head. "You wish."

O'Hara looked back at the woman, who had approached the bar and was now leaning against it. She looked over at O'Hara and Layla and smiled.

"Dina," Layla called out. She then said something in Arabic.

The woman approached them and smiled, and lifted her hand in a slight wave. "*Marhaba*," she said.

"English," Layla said.

"I'm Donovan," O'Hara said.

"Dina," she replied. Up close there was something innocent about her smile, youthful and disarming. But it was her eyes, the pale gray of an early storm cloud, that captured his attention. Something about the intensity of her gaze made him feel exposed, as though she sensed that he had just lied to her.

Layla asked Dina a question in Arabic, to which she nodded. She began mixing her a drink.

"Well," Dina said. "Welcome to Lebanon."

"Thank you," O'Hara replied.

She smiled and glanced toward a table of men getting seated. When she did so, O'Hara noticed a dark scar that ran across her neck beneath her jawline.

Layla placed a drink on the bar.

"Excuse me, I must bring this to a customer," Dina said, and picked up the drink.

"Nice meeting you," O'Hara said.

As Dina walked away, O'Hara snuck a glance at her backside before turning to Layla. "Lebanon," he said, widening his eyes.

Layla laughed. "She is a sweet girl. Too good for this place."

"Is that her man, over there?" O'Hara gestured toward the pretty man.

Layla laughed. "He is a homosexual."

"Oh, good."

She rolled her eyes, and then motioned toward an empty barstool. "Sit. I have to get back to work before Ali gets upset."

O'Hara straddled the stool. She uncorked the bottle of red wine and refilled his glass.

"Cheers," he said.

As Layla tended to a customer at the other end of the bar, O'Hara glanced over his shoulder at the dark corner Ali had first emerged from. He could make out the silhouettes of four other men sitting back there with him. When she returned, he tapped his finger on the bar top to get her attention.

"What's in the back corner?"

"It's where the gangsters hang out when they are here," she said in a low tone without looking up from the bar. She wiped the surface with a towel. "Viktor conducts a lot of his business from back there."

"Is Viktor there now?"

She nodded.

He resisted the urge to turn and look, but wanted to put a face to the name of this dangerous Russian. He wondered how long it would take him to find a reason to interact with the man. He took a swig of wine and watched Dina return to the bar to retrieve another drink order. She glanced over and smiled before ferrying the drinks to a table of older men playing a game of backgammon.

A telephone that hung beside the cash register rang and Layla answered it. She said nothing, but looked back over her shoulder, toward the darkened corner, and nodded her head before placing the phone back on the receiver.

"I will be right back," she said to O'Hara, and walked out from behind the bar and toward the dark corner.

O'Hara was lost in thought among the electronic house melodies that played from the corner speakers. He had an unsettled, restless feeling, as though he were wasting time sitting there. He had to remind himself that his only purpose in entering the bar that night was to hang out and be seen. He felt a tap on his shoulder and turned on his stool to find Dina standing behind him.

"Hey Dina," he said as he turned to face her.

"I am finishing my shift, and will have a drink with my friend Amjad." She pointed toward the table, where the pretty man raised a hand and smiled. "Would you like to join us?"

"I'd like that," O'Hara said. "What are you drinking?"

"We will share a bottle of wine."

"I'll see you over there," he said.

She smiled and walked across the room, exiting through the swinging door.

Layla returned to the bar and began filling a pint glass with beer from the tap. "There's been a change of plans," she said. "Keep looking down at your drink so that it doesn't seem like we are talking to each other."

"What's up?" O'Hara asked.

She looked toward another customer who sat belly-up to the bar. "First, Ali was asking a lot of questions about you. I think he is already jealous."

"Oh well," O'Hara said.

"This is good. We want him interested in you. But he also just told me to make sure all the shelves are stocked with full bottles and to switch out any kegs that are running low." She finished pouring the beer and used a coaster to scrape the excess foam from the top of the glass. "To clear tables for a dance floor, and to expect a crowd."

O'Hara looked up at her. She was still staring at the other customer.

"It means your friend might come earlier than we had anticipated. Last time we created a dance floor, it was for that reason."

O'Hara looked back down at his drink, feeling a sudden urge to leave the bar. For over a month he'd been imagining his first encounter with Red. Visualizing what he would say, how it would play out. A long life of experience taught him that nothing ever went according to plan. But he'd never expected this opportunity to come so soon.

Layla walked down the bar with the beer and placed it in front of a customer. When she made her way back to him, O'Hara gestured over his shoulder with his thumb, toward Amjad's table.

"Let me get a good bottle of red. I'm gonna go have a drink with Dina and her friend."

Layla nodded. "I will bring it over."

O'Hara finished his glass of wine and stood from the stool.

"Do you feel comfortable with your friend coming so soon?" Layla asked.

"Comfortable?" he asked, with a shrug. "I guess tonight's as good as any. Do me a favor and bring a pen over with that wine."

"A pen?"

"Please." O'Hara turned and walked toward the round wooden table that Dina's friend Amjad was sitting behind. He glanced once more at the dark corner and noticed Ali watching him. At this closer distance he was able to make out the man that sat beside Ali. The way the dim lighting of the room cast itself upon his angular features gave his face a skull-like appearance, with shadows collected in deep eye sockets and sunken cheeks. The man then turned his head, revealing the sharp angle of a long, birdlike nose. O'Hara wondered if he might be wearing a disguise of some sort.

He reached the table and nodded at Amjad.

"Please, sit," Amjad said, with a smile, revealing a row of flawless, white teeth.

"Dina invited me over," O'Hara said. "I've got another bottle of vino on its way."

"Yes, of course. Welcome. And thank you for the wine."

O'Hara sat in one of the empty chairs.

"So you are from the States, yes?" Amjad asked.

O'Hara nodded and gestured over his shoulder. "I know Layla from when she was out there, studying. She's been telling me to visit Beirut for the longest time."

"Well, you have made it, *ilhamdulillah*," Amjad said.

"You from around here?"

"No, I am Saudi. I am a student at the university, here."

"Is that how you know Dina?"

Amjad nodded. He gestured beyond O'Hara's shoulder. O'Hara turned to find Dina walking toward the table. She was now dressed in a loosely draped kaftan top and a bohemian style, knit satchel purse hung across her chest from one shoulder. As she sat in an empty chair, Layla arrived with the bottle of wine and three new glasses and set them down on the table.

"Don't be corrupting them," she said to O'Hara.

"If they've survived being around you, they'll be fine."

Layla grinned and uncorked the bottle.

O'Hara picked up the wine and filled everyone's glasses.

Layla pulled a pen from her pocket and handed it to O'Hara, before walking away.

The bouncer had come in from his post outside the front door. He began tipping empty tables onto their sides and rolling them toward the back where he leaned them against a wall. Layla helped clear the chairs.

O'Hara sipped his wine. "So what do you two study at the university?"

"There isn't much going on at the moment, with the weirdness of the pandemic. But like a good Gulf Arab, I study engineering," Amjad said with an amicable frown. "She is the braver one who follows her heart."

O'Hara looked at Dina.

"In case you haven't noticed, he is a joker," she said. "I study anthropology. Mostly to do with indigenous cultures."

"I bet that's interesting," O'Hara said. "I always felt like those primitive cultures were the keepers of all the true wisdom."

"It is nice to hear you say that," she said. "I think this, too. With all of our modernity comes way too much noise and distraction." She nodded toward him. "So, what do you do back in Boston?"

"I was an ironworker."

"You say 'was.' Do you no longer have this job?"

"We'll see." He shrugged. "I wanted to come see what was out here in the rest of the world."

"Have you been to many other countries, before Lebanon?"

O'Hara shook his head. "This was my first stop."

"Where will you travel next?" Amjad asked.

"I haven't really thought that far ahead."

"So you will stay here for some time, then," Dina said.

Amjad grinned.

"I'm just playing it by ear," O'Hara said.

"What does this mean?" Dina asked.

Amjad answered her in Arabic, which caused her to giggle and then look at O'Hara.

"I hope you stay for some time," she said.

O'Hara smiled.

"So, *habibi*, were you and Layla lovers?" Amjad asked. "Is that why you came to Beirut, first stop? For some Moroccan magic?"

When he said this, Dina hissed, and then looked at O'Hara. "He sometimes speaks before he thinks," Dina explained.

"I respect bluntness." O'Hara looked at Amjad. "No, Layla is just my friend." He took a drink of wine. "And to answer your real question. Dina here is my type, not you." O'Hara winked at him, causing both Amjad and Dina to laugh.

Amjad put a hand on Dina's wrist. He looked at O'Hara. "I suppose Dina is the next best option."

Dina hid her face in her hands and shook her head.

"Look, we have embarrassed her," Amjad said, slapping his hand on the table and laughing harder.

Layla returned and topped off each of their glasses from the wine bottle.

"You seem to be settling in well," she said to O'Hara. She looked at the other two. "Now you understand why I stayed friends with him."

"*Ilhamdulillah*," Amjad said, as she walked away.

The front door opened and in walked Ali with six attractive women in tight-fitting dresses. The women surveyed the room, some laughing with one another in an exaggerated manner as if to garner attention before walking up to the bar and taking seats on any available stools.

"Escorts," Amjad said. "Eastern Europeans, definitely."

"Shit, you won't want to go anywhere near that," O'Hara said to him. "Not that you would."

"Not my style," Amjad replied with a grin.

O'Hara turned his attention to Dina. "What's your work schedule like, here?"

"I work two nights each week," she said.

"Maybe you can show me around Beirut, one of these days."

She smiled. "I can do that."

O'Hara moved his wine glass off the napkin it had been resting on, and used the pen Layla had given him to write his cell phone number on it. He slid the napkin toward Dina. "Enter that into your phone."

She fished her cell phone from her satchel.

He turned the napkin so that the numbers were facing her, and she began punching buttons on her phone.

O'Hara felt his phone vibrate in his pocket. He pulled it out and looked at the screen. On it was a text message typed in Arabic script.

"Sometime later, have that translated," she said.

He slipped his phone back into his pocket, then took the napkin with his phone number, and stuffed it into his other pocket. The front door to the bar opened again and O'Hara turned to see a fair-skinned man with a shaved head enter. He was wearing a tight-fitting polo shirt which accentuated his muscular frame. There were tattoos running the length of his forearms. Behind him followed a half-dozen black men, many of whom began immediately mingling with the escorts.

O'Hara checked each of their faces, keeping his own posture at an angle so as not to be recognized. Last to enter the bar, wearing a linen shirt that showed off his athletic physique, was Red. He lingered in the doorway for a moment to converse with the bouncer and then slapped hands with the man.

O'Hara watched out of the corner of his eye, as his old friend approached the bar, stopping to talk with two of the escorts, before ordering a drink from Layla. His old friend certainly looked the part. With his broad chest and thick muscular arms, he was still built the same as when he was scouted by Rutgers University. Exactly what one would imagine a dangerous black militant might look like. A perfect mascot for the Idaho fear-mongering narrative of what would be returning to America to ruin it with terror and violence. O'Hara knew it was just an act, though. He knew the muscles were a front, and how they were enhanced by the tip of a needle. He also knew it was not Red's physicality that needed to be respected most. His true strength lay between his ears.

"You mind if we switch seats, brother?" O'Hara asked Amjad. "I don't like sitting with my back to so many strangers."

"*Tfaddal*," he replied, and stood from his chair, pulling it out for O'Hara to sit.

From his new seat, he had a good view of the room with only a wall behind him. He continued to observe Red, who now leaned against the bar flirting with an escort as some of his friends began pulling others out onto the dance floor.

"These men come in, sometimes. They're American, too."

"Oh yeah?" O'Hara asked.

Dina nodded. "Viktor knows the Russian man that always brings them." She gestured toward the man with the tattooed arms.

O'Hara watched Red walk up to Ali and shake his hand. He then leaned against the wall beside another member of his group. Red's friend wore his hair braided into tight cornrows that extended down the back of his neck. He bobbed his head to the music, occasionally pulling from a bottle of the local Al-Maza beer. He was the only one among Red's crew that had not shown interest in the escorts, and to O'Hara, he displayed the hard look of someone from the streets, or prison.

Ali guided two of the escorts across the room and introduced them to Red and his friend.

"They must be important people, because this is the third or fourth time I have seen them here. And it is always like this, with the escorts and the dance floor and Ali giving them whatever they want."

O'Hara was now feeling the warm effects of the wine, and thought it would be a good idea to slow down his drinking. "What is the link between the black guys and the Russians?"

Dina shrugged and shook her head. "I don't know. I am just a waitress." She finished off the last of the wine in her glass. "Layla would be a better person to ask about that."

O'Hara nodded, but said nothing.

Dina placed a hand on his forearm. "I am very sorry to do this, but I can see Ali looking over here, and I know he will soon ask me to stay and wait tables, now that it has become busy." She stood from her seat. "I should leave, before I get trapped."

"Yeah, you don't want to have to deal with a crowd like this," O'Hara said, glad that she would not be present for what might lie ahead. "Are you alright to get home?"

"Amjad will walk me," Dina said. "If I don't force him to leave now, he will still be here, drunk when the sun rises."

"I am already drunk," Amjad said and turned up his wine glass, finishing what was left with a large swallow.

"Don't forget to translate the message I sent you," Dina said, pointing toward his jeans pocket.

"Will do." O'Hara stood.

She leaned in and kissed him on the cheeks three times.

"We must hang out again," Amjad said to O'Hara from across the table.

"Get my number from Dina," O'Hara said, and held a fist up for Amjad to knock knuckles with, before he might try kissing him as well.

Once they had left, O'Hara kept his head low and walked over to the bar where he ordered a glass of tonic water from Layla. She served it to him with ice and a lemon, making it look like a cocktail. He nursed his drink, killing time while allowing himself to sober up some, and used the mirrored tile backsplash behind the bar to keep an eye on Red. So far, it did not appear his old friend had taken notice of him.

In between serving customers, Layla would stop to chat with O'Hara, but kept the conversations vague and impersonal in case any other customers were eavesdropping. Once he had finished his tonic water, O'Hara put his glass down and turned to face the rest of the room. He leaned his back against the bar and began bobbing his head with the music.

A raven-haired beauty in a short dress, approached him and asked something in what sounded like Russian. She began rubbing his arm and giggling. He smiled and pretended to enjoy her advances, despite not having a clue about what she was saying. He was hoping Red would look over and notice him.

When it finally happened — Red glanced in his direction — they locked eyes. Red looked away, then back at him. This time he held his stare and O'Hara knew he had been recognized. He reached down and tightened his belt a few notches, to ensure that his gun was secured against his waist. He excused himself from the escort and crossed the room, as if heading toward the toilets. As he grew nearer to where Red stood, he knew he was being watched. When they were within a few feet of one another, O'Hara stopped walking and stepped toward him.

"The fuck are you looking at?" he asked Red.

"Whassup, motherfucker?!" asked the hard-looking man with the cornrows, who was standing beside Red. "What you said?" the man added.

Without saying a word, O'Hara hit the man hard on the jaw with an overhand right. His braided head snapped back and his body stiffened for a moment, before collapsing. Red rushed in to tackle O'Hara, who used the momentum to flip him on the way down, causing both men to hit the ground. Commotion erupted in the background.

While grappling one another on the floor, O'Hara could hear shouts and breaking glass. He stuck his hand in his pocket and pulled out the napkin that had his phone number written on it, then stuffed it in the pocket of Red's jeans.

He felt kicks rain down on his back. He let go of Red and scrambled to his feet, eating punches from two men who had swarmed him. He was too close to land clean shots on the nearest man, so he stepped forward and head-butted him on the nose, feeling the bridge give way. The man covered his face with his hands and O'Hara folded him with a liver shot.

O'Hara saw a flash of white light, and was dropped back to his hands and knees by a punch from behind. He heard yelling. Ali, the bouncer, and the man with the tattooed arms were shoving people back and shouting in at least three different languages. Layla rushed toward the middle and ushered O'Hara back toward the bar.

"Are you okay?" she asked him.

"I'm fine."

"You're bleeding," she said, and grabbed a bar towel to wipe blood from his brow.

O'Hara looked back at where the fight had occurred. Red was restrained against the wall by the man with the tattooed arms. An escort was holding a towel to the face of the guy he had head-butted, while the man with the braids was still on the floor being propped up in a sitting position. Ali stood over them all, scanning the room as if searching for something. He stopped when his eyes found Layla and O'Hara.

He yelled at Layla in Arabic, swinging his arms wildly and pointing toward the exit. He then called out to the muscular bouncer, who was holding one of Red's friends in a bear-hug.

The bouncer released the man and walked toward the bar, moving with purpose. "You go!" he yelled at O'Hara, and stepped toward him.

"Fuck off," O'Hara answered.

The man then pointed toward the door. "*Yalla!*"

"Go home," Layla said to O'Hara, in a soft voice. "I will smooth things over and have Omar update you."

O'Hara turned and walked toward the exit. "Get outta my way," he said, as he walked past the bouncer and left the bar.

The streets were dark and deserted on the short walk back to his flat, save for a handful of men that sat outside a cafe, smoking nargila and drinking tea among the steady rumbling of generators that filled the night air. When he reached the building, the lights of the bakery were on, and through the window he could see Anwar and Mona in the back kitchen, moving trays in and out of the ovens. He knocked on the glass and they both looked up. Anwar waved and motioned for Mona to walk out.

She opened the sliding window, and frowned. "Donovan, *ya habibi*, you are bleeding. Come inside," she said, and turned to walk toward the entry door.

"I slipped on the rocks down by the ocean. I am fine, thank you."

Mona held up a finger. "I will get you a wet rag to clean your face."

Before he could protest, she had already walked away. When she returned, she handed him a wet rag through the window opening. "Wipe the blood."

O'Hara did as she suggested, and thanked her.

"I would offer you food, but it is still in the oven, baking."

"That's very kind of you," he replied. "I was actually hoping you could help me with something else." He pulled the phone from his pocket and used the buttons to bring Dina's text message up onto the screen. He handed it through the window. "Would you translate the Arabic for me?"

"Of course," she said, accepting the phone. She looked at the screen for a moment, before a large grin appeared on her face. She looked up at him. "Who's Dina?"

"A friend of mine," he answered.

"It says, I hope that you stay in Lebanon for a long time." Her grin widened. "Dina." She handed the phone back through the window opening.

"Thank you."

"When you marry her, you will invite me and Anwar to the wedding so that we may provide pastries for the guests." She giggled.

O'Hara smiled. Before he could respond, they were interrupted by the haunting call of the fajr azan, echoing off the buildings that lined the street.

"Please excuse me, I must go pray," Mona said.

"Of course. Thanks for your help." He slipped the phone into his pocket, and headed upstairs, to his flat.

CHAPTER FIVE

"Is that your only war wound?" Omar asked, once O'Hara was inside the taxi.

O'Hara touched the small gash near his eye, that had begun to scab. "One of them caught me pretty good," he said.

The Israeli picked up one of two paper coffee cups that were resting in drink holders hanging from his radiator vents, and handed it to O'Hara. "American style, with cream."

"Thanks," O'Hara said, taking the cup and peeling back a strip of the plastic lid with his teeth. He sipped the coffee.

"You broke Dorian Smith's jaw. And Layla said another guy has a shattered nose."

"Smith is the one with the braids?"

Omar nodded. "He now has his mouth wired shut, thanks to you." He turned the corner and drove along the corniche toward the Christian east.

"I needed a way to break the ice."

"You broke more than that." Omar pulled a pack of cigarettes down from where it was held by the overhead sun visor, and shook one loose, drawing it from the box with his teeth. He returned the box to its place and used a plastic lighter to spark the end of the cigarette. He took two rapid puffs and released a cloud of smoke toward the window. "My friend, you are either brilliant, or fucked."

"How so?"

"How are you brilliant? Or how are you fucked?"

"Whichever."

"Well, Layla said Ali is furious."

"That guy's an asshole," O'Hara replied.

"She also said that Viktor now wants to talk to you." He nodded toward the windshield.

"Why?"

"When Viktor says he wants something, nobody asks why. They just make sure he gets it. This is why we are headed to the Achrafieh suburb, now. If he is interested enough to put men out watching you, we don't want them seeing us together."

Omar took a hard drag from his cigarette and blew a stream of smoke out the window. "So far, it has always been the same six men that come to Bar Sofia from the training camps. We believe that they are a small unit who are trained to act as such. Guerrilla tactics. If one of their two leaders now has a wire in his jaw, and if one of the other men has a broken nose and swollen eyes, this will likely delay any sudden attacks on the settlements along the Golan." He returned the coffee to the drink holder. "Maybe it will cause them to cancel the Golan idea entirely, and they will just focus on returning to America." He used his fingers to drum a beat along with the Arabic pop song that was playing from the car stereo.

"I picked that fight in order to get close to Red."

"What do you mean?"

"During the scuffle I stuffed a napkin with my phone number into his pocket." O'Hara raised his cup to his lips. "He'll call." He took a long swig of his coffee.

Omar looked over at O'Hara, grinning. "Maybe you are more brilliant than fucked."

They drove down a street that was lined on one side by a high stucco wall painted with a large mural of the Virgin Mary. Across the street were residential homes with sizable front lawns and colorful gardens, protected by iron gates.

"We will wait and see what happens next. Layla will return to work tonight and will update me on any gossip from the bar." He looked at O'Hara. "Where would you like to be dropped off?"

"Somewhere over on the west side, I guess."

Omar lit another cigarette, then shifted the gears and turned the car out of the quiet lane. O'Hara stared out the window in silence, wondering if Red would bother to contact him.

He was dropped beside a cafe near Martyrs' Square in the central district of the city. He sat at an outdoor table and drank coffee and ate fresh hummus with baked flat bread. Over the nearest rooftop he could see the light blue domes of the Mohammed Al-Amin Mosque, its four towering minarets pointing up into the cloudless sky above, like rockets preparing for launch. He had bought a pair of knock-off sunglasses from a street vendor which he wore to hide the gash and bruising that had developed above his eye.

His phone lay on the table next to his food and he stared at it, trying to think of a clever response he might text Dina. The screen suddenly lit up and the phone vibrated. He picked it up and held it to his ear.

"Hey," he said.

"How are you doing?" Dina asked from the other end of the line.

"Good. I'm just sitting here, eating breakfast close to that big, blue-domed mosque. I was about to reply to your text, actually."

"Did you have it translated?"

"I did." He was smiling.

"What do you think about it?"

"I think that I can be persuaded."

"Great," she replied. "I'm very persuasive."

"What are you up to, today?"

"Well, in normal times the pools at the Riviera Hotel, along the ocean, would host big parties with DJs every Sunday. But, because of the pandemic, you know..."

"That's too bad. Sounds like it would have been a good time."

"But in Beirut we improvise. Amjad has a relative who takes his yacht off the coast and throws even better parties than Riviera did. Would you like to come?"

"If you're going."

"Excellent. If you are near the mosque you are very close to Martyrs' Square. Go there and find the statue. We will meet you there in one hour. Do you know the statue I'm talking about?"

"I'll find it."

"Great. See you there."

O'Hara finished his food and walked to a nearby souvenir shop where he bought a pair of swim shorts and a towel that looked like a Lebanese flag. He then walked around a cobblestone plaza with a large clock tower at its center, lined with restaurants and cafes that were empty of customers. He pulled his phone from his pocket and found Layla's phone number and called her.

"Doni," she answered.

"What's up?"

"Did you see Omar?"

"Yeah. Dina just invited me to some party on a yacht."

"The Sunday yacht parties are the place to be seen in Beirut during the pandemic."

"Will you be going?"

"Yes, but don't wait for me. Go with Dina. I will arrive with Ali."

"Is everything smoothed out with him?" O'Hara asked.

"Everything will be fine. I'll see you at the party."

"Alright. See you there."

"*Salaam*," she said, and disconnected the line.

He slipped the phone back in his pocket and headed toward Martyrs' Square.

* * *

O'Hara could hear the music long before he could see anything up above, on the deck of the yacht. An electronic melody of beats mixed with the occasional long drawn strokes of a violin. The music rode the ocean breeze as a small boat taxied them toward the party. The high sidewalls of the ship were bone white, and rose twenty or thirty feet out of the ocean. Thick links of anchor chain descended into the sea alongside a retractable staircase that had been extended at the rear of the vessel. The occasional wave lapped gently over the landing at its base.

The water taxi was captained by a local fisherman who had been hired by the yacht's owner and paid handsomely to ferry guests from the port of Beirut to the yacht every Sunday. The captain maintained discretion as to exactly where he was taking them.

Dina sat across the aisle from O'Hara with her eyes closed and the ocean wind blowing hair from her face. She had on large aviator sunglasses and a loosely draped linen shirt with shorts and a towel folded across her lap. She wore no makeup, unlike the women that were sitting beside her, who featured a combination of dyed hair, swollen lips and cheekbones that looked like anaphylactic reactions. O'Hara thought in that moment that he may not have known a more beautiful face than Dina's. It was not the beauty inside the glossy pages of magazines, or posing on celebrity red carpets. It was more of the kind which occurs when inner purity manifests itself outward. An organic beauty that both enchanted and disarmed him anytime she looked over and smiled. He had to remind himself that he had not even known this woman twenty-four hours. He knew that if he were not careful he might easily lose sight of his reason for being in Lebanon.

Once close enough, the captain turned off the boat engine and tossed a line to a uniformed man standing on the edge of the yacht's platform, at the base of the white stairs. Amjad and the man were already yelling back and forth to one another in Arabic, laughing, as the man caught the rope and helped guide the small boat near. O'Hara, Dina and Amjad, along with other women, stepped across onto the platform. They climbed the steep stairs, moving toward the melody that played from dozens of mounted speakers running the width of the ship.

The stairs led to the main deck, where a man holding an electronic tablet asked the four women for their names before scanning a list and finding each. He tapped the tablet screen multiple times with his finger, then stepped aside and allowed them to pass. When he saw Amjad he kissed him on both cheeks. He smiled at Dina, and with a slight nod and a wave of his hand, motioned for the three of them to enter.

The rear section of the yacht contained a saltwater pool that was two-thirds the width of the ship and at least a quarter of its length. Scores of lounge chairs lined the edges, where shirtless men and bikini-clad women lay oiled and glistening under the bright sun. A second level contained more guests, some of whom were dancing to the music played by a DJ in a pulpit who overlooked the pool. At the highest levels were enclosed cabins with dark tinted windows, above which a white helicopter was stationed.

"*Yalla,*" Amjad said and walked over to a bar in the corner of the deck, where he ordered three bottles of Al-Maza beer, and handed them out to O'Hara and Dina.

They took their beers to the corner of the pool and draped their towels over three vacant lounge chairs.

"You know the owner of this boat?" O'Hara asked.

"Dirty rich," Amjad said with a smile. "Isn't this an American slang?"

"Filthy rich?"

"Yes, that." Amjad sipped his beer. "He is my cousin."

"What's he do for a living?"

"Nothing, *habibi.* He is a prince."

"A what?"

"There are hundreds of princes in Saudi. It's not like the Prince of Wales."

"Does that make you a prince, then? Being his cousin?"

Amjad forced an uncomfortable laugh. "Definitely not."

O'Hara pulled his shirt off over his head. He noticed Dina looking at the worm-like scar that ran across the right side of his chest, where he had once been cut in a fight on Rikers Island.

She unbuttoned her linen shirt and slipped out of it, turning away to hang it over the backrest of her lounge chair. She then unhooked the clasp of her shorts and let them fall to her ankles, causing O'Hara's heart to skip a beat.

Amjad laughed when he noticed where O'Hara's eyes were focused. "I like your tattoos," he said to O'Hara. He had stripped down to a small, Speedo swimsuit.

"Thanks." He nodded toward Amjad's swimsuit. "I like your pud purse."

Dina giggled. She sat in her lounge chair and reclined.

"Not everyone can pull these off so well," Amjad said with an exaggerated lisp.

As he leaned back in his chair, O'Hara noticed another Caucasian man across the pool, dressed in a pale purple shirt and khaki shorts. He was taller than average and thinly built, like an endurance athlete, and had short brown hair that was kept from his face by a pair of sunglasses resting on top of his head. As the man crossed the deck, making his way toward the stairs that led to the upper level, he stopped to shake hands with multiple groups of people that were sitting poolside.

O'Hara pushed his sunglasses up on his forehead to wipe a bead of sweat from the corner of his eye. When he did this, Dina looked over.

"How's your cut?" she asked.

"It's just a nick," O'Hara said, and sipped his beer.

Amjad laughed.

"What?" O'Hara asked.

"It's just that 'nick' means something else in Arabic."

Some of the guests were now wading in the shallow end of the pool, drinks in hand. O'Hara noticed the women that had arrived on the water taxi with them, now flirting with a group of bearded men.

"Do you know a lot of the guests, here?"

"I know many of the faces," Amjad said. "But I do not know them all by name."

"Is your cousin among them?"

Amjad gestured his head toward the tinted windows of the highest cabin, just below the helicopter. "I will go see him if he sends for me." He sipped his beer. "He usually conducts business meetings throughout the day, since he is only here once a week."

"Does he not live here?"

Amjad shook his head. "He flies in from Riyadh on Sundays." He then pointed toward the back wall of the deck, where Ali stood, shaking hands with some of the yacht staff members. He was wearing an open dress shirt with a tank top beneath it, and white suit pants with loafers.

"Guess Ali's too cool for swimming," O'Hara said.

A moment later Layla appeared at the top of the stairs behind Ali. Her hair was tightly braided into two long tails behind her head, and she wore designer sunglasses and a beach dress that hung loosely over a bikini. Together, they looked like a pretentious couple from the Hamptons or South Beach. She noticed O'Hara and waved, then walked in his direction. Ali followed behind her.

When she arrived, she greeted each of them with kisses.

"How is your eye?" she asked O'Hara.

"All good," O'Hara replied, and raised his sunglasses to allow her to see the wound.

Ali stepped forward. "I need to talk to you," he said to O'Hara in a stern voice.

"Here I am," O'Hara replied. "Talk."

"No, we will talk in private."

O'Hara sipped his beer and said nothing.

"I explained to Ali that his guests started the confrontation, last night," Layla said, and placed a gentle hand on Ali's shoulder.

Ali clucked his tongue. "I said I will talk to him in private." He snapped his finger at a passing yacht crew member and said something in Arabic. "Cigar?" he asked O'Hara.

"Why not?" O'Hara replied.

Ali held up two fingers, to which the crew member nodded. Ali then looked at O'Hara. "When the cigars arrive, bring them up to the next level and find me."

O'Hara did not acknowledge his command. He watched as Ali walked away beneath the DJ booth and toward the staircase in the back corner. Layla slipped her dress off and sat on an empty lounge chair beside him.

"He wanted to have you hurt, but Viktor stopped it." Layla was talking in a near whisper, so that Dina and Amjad would not hear.

"Omar said that Viktor wants to see me."

Layla nodded. "I have yet to figure out why."

"Did Red mention anything about recognizing me?"

Layla clucked her tongue. "He just said you hit his friend for no reason at all."

The crew member returned holding two Cuban cigars. "I'll take those, thanks," O'Hara said and stood, accepting the cigars from the man. He looked at the others. "See you in a bit," he said, and walked to one of the bars where he ordered another beer, before heading upstairs.

The sundeck above was blanketed with a manicured turf lawn and at its center, a group of bikini-clad women danced barefoot to the music as men lined the edges, holding drinks or smoking cigarettes. O'Hara located Ali standing off in one corner, leaning his elbows against the guardrail as he looked out over the crowded swimming pool.

O'Hara walked up beside him and held out a cigar. Ali accepted it, and pulled a metal lighter from his pocket, along with a cigar cutter. He had yet to speak as he used the cutter to slice off the end of his cigar, then handed it to O'Hara, who did the same. Ali snapped open the hinged lid of the metal lighter, lit the end of his cigar and took a few puffs. He handed O'Hara the lighter and exhaled a cloud of smoke in his direction.

"What happened at my bar last night?" Ali asked, as O'Hara lit his own cigar.

O'Hara puffed on the cigar, and blew smoke from the side of his mouth. "If you blow smoke in my face again, the same thing might happen to you."

Ali smirked.

O'Hara cleared his throat and spit off the edge of the boat, then drank from his beer.

"I was going to have you kidnapped and beaten," Ali said. He held his cigar up near his mouth, as if he were going to smoke it, but then paused. He gestured toward the pool, below. "Layla persuaded me not to."

O'Hara grinned, aware that he was bluffing. That it was Viktor who stopped him.

Ali pointed to the scar on O'Hara's chest. "What happened there?"

"Why am I up here talking to you?" O'Hara asked, ignoring the question.

"Layla said the black Americans started the fight with you."

"It's true."

"Their version of the story is very different." When O'Hara did not speak, he pressed his index finger against O'Hara's chest.

O'Hara looked down at his chest. Ali let his hand fall.

"So now I am left with the problem of what to do with you. You disrespected my place of business, and therefore disrespected me. So the way I see things, you are now in debt to me."

"I don't owe you shit."

The smirk returned to Ali's face. "You're in Lebanon, my friend. We don't play by the rules of Boston." He held his arm out over the rail, and used his finger to flick ash from his cigar. "So yes, you do owe me."

O'Hara studied him for a long moment. "What do you need from me?"

"Layla told me you left America because of some trouble you had gotten into?"

O'Hara looked away.

"What kind of trouble?"

"Do I seem like the type of guy that will answer that?"

Ali studied O'Hara's eyes, as if he was searching for signs of dishonesty. "I will think of a way you can repay me for the headache you have caused me."

"You do that," O'Hara replied.

A wide grin appeared on Ali's face.

"Are we done, here?" O'Hara asked.

When Ali did not respond, O'Hara turned to walk away.

"One last thing," Ali said.

O'Hara stopped and looked back.

"Be careful with how you treat my girls."

O'Hara laughed and shook his head as he walked away. As he neared the stairs that led down to the pool level, the tall Caucasian man in the purple shirt was climbing the steps. As they passed one another they made eye contact, and the man nodded. O'Hara returned a nod, then stopped and leaned his back against the railing, as if to finish his smoke. He watched as the man walked over to the bar, ordered two mixed drinks from the bartender and then carried them over to the corner where Ali was still standing, looking out over the pool.

O'Hara watched the man hand one of the drinks to Ali. He then descended the stairs before either of them had the chance to look in his direction. Downstairs, Dina was the only one of their group still sunning herself on the lounge chairs.

"Where's Amjad?" he asked Dina.

Her eyes had been shut behind her sunglasses.

"He went up to see his cousin," she said.

He sat down beside her. The alcohol mixed with the tobacco had him feeling a bit lightheaded. He lay back on his lounge chair and closed his eyes, allowing the wind off the ocean to cool his skin.

"I've gotta get something off my chest," he said.

"What does this mean?" she asked.

O'Hara made a sweeping motion with his arm, across the width of the swimming pool. "I see the way the men here look at you. How they looked at you at the bar last night." He smiled. "I'll be honest. I'm having a hard time understanding how you don't have a man."

She smiled and turned her head away as if embarrassed, then looked back at him. "I was raised well. I don't just go with men, the way some of these women do." She nodded toward the water, where three women were hanging on the shoulders of a group of handsome men. "This playboy behavior does not impress me."

"What does impress you?"

"Authenticity."

O'Hara held his beer out in her direction. She raised her bottle and touched it to his.

"To the people who raised you that way."

When he said this, he noticed her expression soften.

"Do they live in Beirut?"

She clucked her tongue. "They still own the home I was raised in. In Zahle. But they live in Paris."

"Paris? Wow." He sipped his beer. "Where's Zahle?"

"It is to the east, toward Syria. Some call it the city of wine and poetry. I should take you there sometime."

"I'd love that," he responded.

"Then I will." She winked.

A phone began to ring somewhere nearby. It was not until O'Hara felt the vibration against his leg, that he realized it was his own cell phone. He pulled it from his pocket and looked at it, not recognizing the number on the screen. "Excuse me, just a sec," he said.

She leaned back in her lounge chair as he stood and walked toward the edge of the deck, bringing the phone to his ear. "Hello," he said.

"Who's this?" a voice asked, in English.

"You called me," O'Hara replied.

"O," the man said.

O'Hara did not reply.

"It's Red."

"Where are you?"

"I don't have much time to talk. You done fucked up last night."

"Save all that bullshit. Whose phone are you calling from?"

"A burner. I stole it off a table in a cafe. The guys I'm with think I'm taking a shit. It'll be one and done on this number."

O'Hara turned around and leaned his back against the railing. He looked up toward the deck where Ali and the Caucasian man were no longer standing.

"We need to meet," O'Hara said.

"You need to tell me what the fuck you're doing in Lebanon."

"I will when we meet."

"I won't be down to Beirut again for a while, after the shit you pulled in that bar."

"Doesn't have to be Beirut. When can you meet?"

"Hard to tell."

"I know you're in the Bekaa Valley."

"How the hell you know that?"

"Doesn't matter." O'Hara looked over at Dina, who mouthed that she was going for a swim. He nodded at her. "How far are you from a town called Zahle?"

"No clue."

"Fuck it, just pick a time and a place and I'll make it there."

"I'll call you later in the week."

"Cool." O'Hara hung up the phone. He walked back to the lounge chairs, slipped the phone into his shoe and covered it with his towel. He then walked over to the pool, dove into the brisk water, and swam to where the girls were gathered.

"I like this DJ," he said, making small talk to conceal that his attention had been drawn to the edge of the pool, where he noticed the tall Caucasian man easing himself into the water.

"He is from Romania," Dina replied. "He's one of the most famous in the world."

"I bet it cost a fortune to get him out here, with all the travel restrictions."

"Gulf money," Layla said with a laugh.

"Yeah, no kidding."

O'Hara watched the tall man wade through the water in their direction until he was just beyond Layla's shoulder.

"How's it going?" the man asked O'Hara when their eyes met.

O'Hara replied with a nod.

"American?" the man asked.

"I am."

Layla and Dina moved aside to make room for the man.

"Billy Richter," the man said, and extended his hand toward O'Hara.

"Donovan Burke," he replied, clasping the man's hand. "This is Layla and Dina."

"I've seen you both, around. How do you do?" He then looked back at O'Hara. "Where are you from?"

"Boston."

"Beantown? What's got you out here?"

O'Hara nodded at Layla. "Met this one in a bar back home."

"I thought you guys called them *bahs*," Richter said, mocking a Boston accent.

"Did you?" O'Hara asked. "Where're you from?"

"Arizona. So, are you just here visiting Layla, then?"

"Yeah," O'Hara said.

"What do you girls do in Beirut?" Richter asked.

"We're students. And we work at Bar Sofia."

"I know the place."

"What about you?" O'Hara asked the man. "What's got an Arizona boy living out here in Lebanon?"

"I'm a consular officer with the Department of State."

"Sounds important."

Richter laughed. "Don't let the title fool you. I spend most of my time approving and denying visa applications. Mostly denying, these days."

"I bet," O'Hara said.

Dina tapped O'Hara on the shoulder, and when he looked at her, she gestured behind him. He turned around and saw one of the yacht's crew members standing by the side of the pool with what appeared to be a folded towel in one arm.

"Sir, you are requested in the quarters of the *Emir*," the man said, and gestured with an open hand toward the upper cabins of the ship.

"Me?" O'Hara asked.

"Yes, sir," the man said. "Mister Amjad is up there, as well."

O'Hara looked at Dina. "I guess I'll be back in a few." He said it casually, so his voice didn't betray the tension he felt in his gut. He climbed out of the pool and walked over to his lounge chair.

The crew member followed him over and handed him what turned out to be a folded bathrobe. "You are asked to please wear this up there."

O'Hara accepted the robe and let it fall open. He slipped his arms into it and pulled it over his shoulders, then tied it closed by the belt. "How do I get up there?" he asked.

The man pointed toward the back wall, beneath the overhead deck. "There is an elevator. Take it to the top floor."

"Thank you," O'Hara replied.

The man nodded, and walked off.

O'Hara took his cell phone from his shoe and slipped it into the pocket of his robe. He then made his way toward the elevator.

* * *

The polished gold doors parted to reveal a large, oval-shaped room covered by thick, white carpet. Two guards stood on either side of the doorway facing him. Two more men, dressed in starched white robes, were arranging porcelain bowls of food atop a marble buffet table. At the center of the room were three leather armchairs. Amjad sat in one. In the chair beside him, sat a man that did not look much older. He was dressed in a white robe and wore a red checkered *ghutra* head scarf, which was kept in place by double ringed *iqal.* They were both holding glass mugs of tea.

" *Tfaddal*," the man called out across the room, and gestured toward the remaining, empty chair with a large smile.

O'Hara approached them.

"Please, sit," the man requested, speaking English this time.

"Donovan Burke, this is my cousin, Prince Ahmed," Amjad said.

"It's a pleasure to meet you, Prince," O'Hara said.

"Likewise, Mister Burke," the prince replied in a British accent. "Welcome."

"Thank you," O'Hara said, and sat in the empty chair. "When guys back home say they own a boat, they're talking about something that might fit five or six people."

The prince laughed. "I like to help the people of Beirut during this difficult year. It is good for everyone's mental health. Music, water, sun, without all the masks and the restrictions."

O'Hara nodded.

"Amjad speaks very highly of you."

"I appreciate that," O'Hara said to Amjad.

The prince touched his finger to the side of his face. "What is this from?"

"I was welcomed to Beirut by some men, last night."

"Yes, you must be careful in this city. I tell this to Amjad often." The prince looked at his cousin. "Especially with his disposition." He then looked at O'Hara.

O'Hara nodded.

"It does not bother you, I assume."

"Why would it?"

The prince nodded. "In our country this is frowned upon."

Amjad looked down at his lap.

"Amjad is my friend," O'Hara told the prince. "How he lives his life is his business."

Amjad looked up at him.

The prince looked at Amjad, then at O'Hara. He then pointed an open hand toward the table with the food. "Are you hungry? It is all Kentucky."

"Pardon?"

"All the food is from KFC."

"Come on."

The prince nodded. "Fast food, I believe you call it in the States. It is a habit that I picked up from the Crown Prince." He then said something in Arabic to the men that were standing near the table, causing them to begin loading chicken and sides onto empty plates. "So you are from Boston, yes?"

O'Hara nodded.

"What do you do for work, there?"

"I worked construction."

"Well, you will have Amjad let me know if you are ever in need of this type of work while you are out here. I own a company that is currently building in three countries."

"I appreciate the offer, Prince Ahmed."

The prince nodded. "I just wanted to meet you and welcome you to my boat, after hearing that you traveled all the way from the States. Unfortunately, I must excuse myself, now. I am flying to Cairo to watch a football match." He stood.

O'Hara and Amjad both stood.

"Do you like football, Mr. Burke?"

"I do," O'Hara responded.

"I believe we will end up purchasing Newcastle United in the near future. Maybe you will come attend a match with Amjad, if that happens." The prince then gestured toward the two men that were each carrying plates, loaded with food. "Please eat as much as you would like, and enjoy the rest of the party." He said something to Amjad, who walked with him toward a spiral stairwell that led up through the ceiling, at the far end of the room.

When Amjad returned, he took a plate of food and sat.

"You barely said a word," O'Hara commented, accepting a plate of food from one man.

"I must be on good behavior. Some years ago Prince Ahmed took a huge chance in protecting me. Otherwise I might not have a head attached to my shoulders, right now."

"What are you talking about?"

Amjad leaned in closer and lowered his voice. "I can say this to a westerner. I was photographed in bed with a man."

"Who took the picture?"

Amjad shrugged. "Hidden camera."

O'Hara whistled.

"The man I was photographed with was executed. They fabricated a crime and found him guilty." Amjad gestured toward the direction the prince had left. "Prince Ahmed appealed to the Crown Prince, who had known me as a child and who agreed to have me sent abroad, to pursue my studies and live quietly."

"The Crown Prince, himself, did that?"

Amjad nodded.

"Friends in big places, huh?"

"It was because of Prince Ahmed that he did this. They are very close to one another."

"Will they let you go home once you finish school?"

"Saudi?" Amjad asked. He then shrugged as he handed his plate to one of the robed waiters. He stood from the chair. "The Crown Prince will decide that when the time comes."

O'Hara took a final bite of chicken and handed the second waiter his plate.

"Let's go down to the pool and find your girlfriend," Amjad said with a grin.

* * *

When they returned to the pool deck, Dina and Layla had towels wrapped around their torsos and were lounging on the chairs, drinking Al-Maza with Ali and Billy Richter. Amjad ordered two beers from the bar and handed one to O'Hara.

The sun had begun its descent, highlighting the ripples along the ocean in shades of gold and red. Much of the crowd that had been gathered in and around the swimming pool had since moved to the upper deck, where they danced to the progressive house melodies and thumping bass that fit the Mediterranean setting like a movie soundtrack.

"Holding court with the prince," Ali said to O'Hara in a patronizing tone.

"He's the one with the connections," O'Hara said, and hit Amjad's arm.

"The *shez* connection," Ali said. "I bet the Emir loved you," he added, nodding at O'Hara.

O'Hara looked at Amjad, who feigned a look of discomfort. He then looked back at Ali. "You know, you're a prick," he said.

Dina and Layla fought back smiles.

"Be very careful," Ali said.

"Yeah, yeah. I know. This isn't Boston, it's Beirut." O'Hara batted his hand at the air. He looked at Dina. "Wanna take one last dip in the pool?"

"Sure," she replied.

The water was cold, and refreshing, and helped O'Hara clear some of the haze that had gathered in his head from the alcohol. They swam to the deep end of the pool, and treaded water beside one another.

"I'm tired of being around jackasses like Ali. What'll it take to spend some time with just you?"

She smiled when he said this. A purple glow now filled the sky to the east, and the first few stars revealed themselves overhead. Out on the horizon there were still slivers of pale blue behind the sun, which hovered just above the ocean.

"Do you ever wonder what else is out there?" Dina asked, and gestured toward the sky.

"I imagine something must be. We can't be the only ones."

"We aren't." She swam to where she could stand, and he followed her.

"You say that with confidence." O'Hara moved closer to her.

"I feel a bit drunk," she said. "Should we go to Zahle next weekend? The stars there look like you can reach up and touch them."

"I think we should," he replied.

"You think?" she mocked him.

"I think you should let me kiss you."

She did not respond. The last rays of the sun illuminated her face and caused her eyes to glow, as if from within. O'Hara leaned in until their lips met. Under the water, he placed his hands on her hips.

"I was wondering when we would meet," she whispered into his ear.

CHAPTER SIX

He woke early to the sound of the azan echoing through his open window. The red sun had yet to reveal itself, but beams of light shone among mountain peaks to the east and cast shadows along the quiet street below.

Sitting on his patio with a mug of Turkish coffee in his hand, he could see a slice of the sea between two apartment buildings that stood down the hill. He watched the slow drift of the water, and noticed fishermen casting lines from the flat rock formations that extended from the coast, below the corniche. The smells rising from the bakery stirred up cravings that he knew he should earn the right to satisfy. Finishing his coffee, he walked inside, put on a pair of sneakers that Omar had left him, and walked downstairs. He jogged through the streets of Ras Beirut, past Bar Sofia, before turning down toward the corniche. He ran past the port, where large freighters were docked, and shipping containers lined the harbor in rows. He continued along the promenade until he passed the cliffs above Pigeon Rocks, where he then descended the rock face to a barren pebble beach.

The only possessions he had brought with him were his apartment keys and the clothes on his back, so he found a place among bushes to stash his shirt and sneakers, tucking his keys within them. He swam for over an hour. Returning to shore, he was tired and clear-headed.

A few hours later, he met Dina at an outdoor cafe on Bliss street. Across the road, among the gated grounds of the university campus, the iconic clock tower stood tall against a cloudless sky. As they sat and ate crepes and drank from small mugs of espresso, O'Hara reached out and touched the back of her hand.

"I've been thinking a lot about yesterday," he said.

"Me too," she replied.

"Tell me what you meant when you said you were wondering when we'd meet?"

She had been deflecting his questions since having said it, blaming the alcohol for causing her to speak nonsense.

Dina averted her eyes. "I told you, I was in the moment. Feeling vulnerable." She then looked at him and shook her head. "You will think I'm crazy."

"Were you told by someone that you and I would meet?"

She looked down at her plate. "Kind of."

A cold, panic flooded his stomach. "Who, Layla?"

She shook her head, and then released a nervous giggle. "Never mind."

"Who then?" he asked.

"If I tell you something, do you promise not to judge me?"

"Of course," he said.

She inhaled deeply before speaking. "I have these dreams. Very vivid ones."

She nodded. "I have been having them since I was a child. I receive messages. My mother used to tell me that my grandmother had the same gift of dreaming. She could read a person's future in the bottom of a coffee cup." She paused. "Anyway, as I have grown older, the messages in my dreams have become more clear to understand. Now, sometimes I don't even need to be asleep to receive them. They sometimes come to me in daydreams."

"What kind of messages are we talking about?"

"It depends. Sometimes simple ones. Confirmations, or validations of ideas I already have. But, other times they have a deeper meaning. Predictions of things that occasionally will then happen in life. Or messages about the universe and our existence. Things like that."

"You dreamed that we would meet?"

"I believe so." She nodded. "I had a dream about two months ago, where I received the message that I was going to meet someone."

A wide grin appeared on O'Hara's face.

"See, you think I am crazy."

"No, not at all," he protested. "How did you receive this message?"

"There is usually this being, made completely of bright light. So bright I can barely look at her, directly."

"Her?"

"She feels feminine. And she is almost mischievous in her behavior, and always wants me to follow her places. Eventually she allows me to catch up to her and when I do, the whole dream becomes consumed by her light. As if it expands and fills the surrounding space. Then I am often left with some type of message. It isn't something I hear her say. It is more as if the message is implanted in me. Or maybe unlocked from within me.

When I awoke from this one dream, I had a lingering image in my mind of the Statue of Liberty, you know with the New York City skyline behind it, like you see in so many photos. It was random. It's not as if I had been thinking of America or anything like this. But the image was so vivid. So I had this feeling that maybe she was telling me I would go there. Or that I would meet someone from there."

Hearing her mention New York caused a chill to settle at the small of his back.

"I bet I'm that someone," he said.

She smiled and squeezed his hand.

"You should ask your light-being friend if it's me."

She laughed. "It doesn't work that way. I don't ask."

O'Hara savored his espresso. "It's gotta be me."

"I hope so."

*   *   *

He stopped at a Beirut landmark restaurant called Bar Bar, where he ate a chicken sandwich smeared with hummus and drank a glass bottle of cola before making the short walk over to Bar Sofia. There, the musclebound bouncer unlocked the front door and let him inside. The bar had yet to open for business and none of the employees were present. The room was dark, except for a strip of recessed lighting that ran behind the bar, and a single dim bulb that cast a hazy glow over the raised platform in the far corner.

O'Hara could see Viktor sitting there, wearing a black shirt, with the sleeves pushed back to his elbows. The gaunt features of his face cast shadows under the overhead lighting. O'Hara couldn't tell from across the room whether the man's eyes were even open, until he raised a hand and motioned for him to approach. O'Hara took another look around the room to be sure they were alone, and walked toward him.

When he reached the back corner, O'Hara climbed the few steps up onto the platform. Viktor was sitting with his arms outstretched and his palms flat on the tabletop. His forearms were covered with tattoos of a nude woman, a tiger's head, and words written in the Cyrillic alphabet. His head and face were both clean shaven, and with his cadaverous physique, he could have passed for having a terminal illness. His eyes, however, suggested that he was not one to be underestimated. O'Hara had seen eyes like that in prison, among the murderers and the lifers. The cold soulless stare that seemed to look through a person in a penetrating, violating way.

On the table was a bottle of vodka, two empty shot glasses and a pistol. The muzzle was pointed at the empty chair, that Viktor then motioned for O'Hara to sit in.

He sat, ignoring the gun as a drop of sweat ran between his shoulder blades. For what felt like minutes Viktor stared at him and said nothing.

"I know you have a gun," he eventually said in a thick accent. "Take the magazine out and place it all on the table."

O'Hara pulled the Glock from the small of his back and used his thumb to eject the magazine. He placed it on the table.

"The chamber?" Viktor asked.

O'Hara turned the gun so that the muzzle was facing to the side, and he cocked back the slide, causing the final bullet to drop onto the table. He laid his gun down beside the magazine and the lone round.

"Are you a part of a criminal organization in Boston?"

O'Hara shook his head.

"Do not lie to me."

"I'm not."

Viktor picked up the bottle of vodka and uncapped it. He poured a small amount in each of the shot glasses, and slid one toward O'Hara. "Drink."

O'Hara lifted his glass, and waited for Viktor to do the same. They each drank their shots.

"The men you fought here were guests of mine."

"I apologize for the disturbance," O'Hara said. The vodka brought a warmth to his chest.

"Why did it happen?"

"One of them wouldn't stop staring at me."

"And so you attacked him?"

"No, I asked him why he was looking at me."

"And then?"

"I attacked him."

Viktor paused, and pulled a pack of clove cigarettes from his pocket. He made a slow, ritualistic show of pulling a black cigarette from the box, tapping it on the table top, filter down, and then sticking it between his lips. He left the box on the table and retrieved a zippo lighter from his pocket. He lit the end of the cigarette, keeping his eyes focused on O'Hara the entire time. He drew hard on the cigarette, and released clouds of smoke with his words. "So you did not worry about the consequences of creating a disturbance in my bar? Or of harming one of my guests?"

"I was under the impression this was Ali's bar. And I did not realize the men were special guests."

"And if you had known?"

"Which part?"

"That the bar belonged to me."

"With what I know now, I would not have fought."

Viktor picked up the vodka bottle and refilled the shot glasses. "What do you know about me?"

"Just what I have been told."

"Which is what?"

"That you are Russian. And you are a dangerous man."

Viktor gestured toward the glasses. "Drink."

They both turned up their glasses and drank the vodka.

"How do you know Layla?" Viktor asked.

"I met her while she was studying in Boston."

"Have you slept with her?"

"We are just friends."

"You did not answer my question."

"No."

Viktor called out in Arabic to the bouncer, who was sitting on a stool across the room. The man walked over carrying a glass ashtray, and placed it on the table, before returning to his perch. Viktor tapped his cigarette with his finger, letting the ash fall onto the tray.

"Have you noticed I am here alone?" he asked. He gestured across the room. "Other than that useless ape."

"I noticed."

"Do you know why that is?"

O'Hara shook his head.

"Because, if I decided to kill you, I would be the one to do it."

"Why would you kill me?"

"I said if." He rested his half-smoked cigarette against the ashtray. "I would need no one else to do it for me."

"I respect that."

"I have decided that I like the way you handled yourself the other night. Alone. Outnumbered."

O'Hara did not respond.

"I won't kill you."

O'Hara picked up the vodka bottle and filled the shot glasses. "To you not killing me."

Viktor raised his glass, and for the first time since O'Hara had arrived, he grinned. They drank the shots.

"I will give you a job to do. And if you do it well, I will find more work for you."

"Will doing this job clear my debt to Ali?"

Viktor narrowed his eyes. "What debt do you owe Ali?"

"He hasn't told me, yet."

Viktor, made a humming sound. "You owe Ali nothing."

O'Hara nodded.

"You will go to a town called Monsef," Viktor said. "You will meet a Serbian man." Viktor stubbed out the cigarette he had going, pulled another from the pack, and stuck it between his teeth. "You will deliver money to this man and he will have a truck waiting for you. You will drive this truck to an address in Jounieh." He picked up the lighter and lit the end of his cigarette.

"That's it?" O'Hara asked.

"Yes."

"And who do I meet at the second address?"

"Me."

O'Hara nodded. "When do you need me to do this?"

"Thursday." He reached his arm down below the table and pulled up what looked like a small canvas tool bag. He rested the bag on the table. "This is the money you will deliver to the Serb. Written on a piece of paper inside are both the Monsef and the Jounieh addresses. If this money goes missing, or if the truck is not delivered to me in Jounieh. I will kill you."

O'Hara had dealt with criminals and gangsters throughout his life, but he had never before felt such discomfort as in that moment, sitting across from Viktor.

"You will be paid when the truck is delivered to Jounieh."

"Alright." O'Hara stood. "I'm going to load my gun now."

Viktor nodded, and watched as O'Hara slid the magazine back in place and chambered a round, before ejecting the magazine a second time. He picked up the lone bullet that was on the table and loaded it into the top of the magazine, and slid it back into the Glock until he felt it lock in place. He tucked the gun in his pants at the small of his back.

"Are we done here?"

Viktor nodded. "I don't need to see you again until Thursday, in Jounieh."

O'Hara picked up the canvas bag of money from the table.

"Thursday," O'Hara repeated, before walking away.

* * *

A few minutes later O'Hara was walking alongside the iron fence that bordered the American University when a taxi pulled up curbside. He peered through the rolled up window at Omar, then opened the door and climbed in the passenger's seat.

"So this truck..." Omar asked as he pulled the Peugeot into traffic. He beat the horn on the steering wheel to clear the lane ahead. "Did he tell you what will be in it?"

"No. Why?"

"Ali told Layla that someone very important will visit Beirut this weekend."

"Who?"

"He did not say, but from the way everybody seems to be preparing we think it could be the fat man."

"The fat man?"

"Nikolai Semenov."

"Who's that?"

Omar beat a rhythm out on the car horn and changed lanes. "He is on your FBI's most wanted list."

"An associate of Viktor's?"

"They are not in the same league. Viktor is just a dangerous thug who murdered his way to a position of power. Semenov is the type of gangster that finances war zones in third world countries."

"I see," O'Hara said, wondering what he had taken on by agreeing to the job.

Omar pulled the car over a few blocks away from Martyrs' Square.

"So, Thursday," O'Hara said, and climbed out of the car and shut the door.

CHAPTER SEVEN

On Thursday morning they drove north, across the once-Biblical landscape of rolling, cedar-speckled hills to one side and tranquil ocean on the other, passing through stretches where villas dotted the hills above, as well as downtrodden villages where cramped homes looked on the verge of collapse. In one slum they passed through, O'Hara noticed a family with young children searching through a dumpster of trash behind a grocery store. Omar called out the names of the more attractive cities and towns as they drove. Jounieh. Byblos. Monsef.

He pulled the taxi over beside a closed down fuel station in Monsef and let O'Hara out. "The bar is a few hundred feet behind us," he said.

O'Hara nodded and pretended to lean back into the car to pay Omar the taxi fare, before closing the door and walking away. The Peugeot pulled back on to the road and disappeared around the next corner. Carrying the canvas bag Viktor had given him, he crossed to the coastal side of the street and walked south past what appeared to be a hotel to a sign that read Beach Bar in both English and Arabic script.

Stone steps descended to a landing where rows of cushioned lounge chairs overlooked an ocean inlet that was enclosed on three sides by rock walls. Seawater entered through a break in the rocks to form a tide pool under a steel pedestrian bridge, from which hammock chairs hung down to the water at the end of long ropes. A middle-aged couple lay asleep, sunbathing on two of the lounge chairs. The only other person present was a light-skinned man with a shaved head, wearing designer sunglasses and leaning against a wall covered by a graffiti mural of a blue siren's head. When O'Hara looked his way, he raised an arm in acknowledgement, and both men began walking toward one another.

The man extended his hand as they met, and O'Hara clasped it. The man said something in Arabic, then Russian.

"English," O'Hara replied.

"Okay," the man replied. He was holding a cigarette in his other hand, and brought it to his mouth and took a drag. "I am Vidic," he added, with an accent that O'Hara would not have recognized had he not already been told the man was Serbian.

"Donovan."

"How do you know Viktor?"

"From Beirut," O'Hara replied.

"But you speak no Arabic?"

O'Hara shook his head.

"Where are you from?"

"America."

Vidic nodded. "Do you want a drink?"

"I'm okay, thanks."

"Then we will go," Vidic said, and placed a hand on O'Hara's shoulder while pointing up the stone stairs with the hand that held his cigarette.

O'Hara followed him up the stairs to the street level, where they both climbed into a white Range Rover. Vidic drove inland, past expensive looking homes and cross-topped churches, until they reached a large property that was surrounded by black iron gates, at least ten feet tall. Within the gates sat a large cream-colored stucco villa with a red tiled roof. During the short drive from the Beach Bar, Vidic had not said a word. When they reached the electronic gate at the front of the property, he turned to O'Hara.

"Do you want to fuck?" he asked, in a nonchalant manner.

"What the hell did you just say?" O'Hara asked him. He tried to appear unfazed by the question. He unclipped his seatbelt, wondering if he would be better off hitting the man or drawing his gun.

"I have three whores, here. If you want to fuck one, you may."

"Thanks," O'Hara replied, feeling relief. "But I should probably get back on the road."

"Is that a yes or a no?" the man asked. "I keep them drugged. You can do anything you want to them."

"I'm good, thanks." Hearing this, he would have rather put a bullet in the man's head.

"You're good," Vidic replied, in a way that made O'Hara think his words were misunderstood.

"No, thank you," he clarified.

Vidic shrugged and leaned his arm out the window and punched a code on the buttons of a keypad mounted at the top of a pole. The heavy gate began to slide open. They drove down a paved path that extended a few hundred feet before wrapping around a stone fountain with a statue of an archer, aiming a bow and arrow as if to shoot the sky.

"This is a beautiful property," O'Hara said. "Do you live here all year?"

"Here and Belgrade."

Vidic parked the Range Rover and the two of them climbed out. Vidic removed the bag of money from the rear seat and paused.

"Are you sure you will not fuck? You can have Bulgarian, Syrian, Vietnamese."

"I'm just gonna take the truck and get going." It took effort not to bash the man.

Vidic studied his face for a moment, with an expression of disbelief, and then nodded. "Okay," he said, and walked over to a large garage door and punched buttons on a keypad that was mounted to one side. He stepped back as the door began to rise, revealing a white, box delivery truck, parked within.

"Do you know where you are driving it to?" Vidic asked.

O'Hara nodded, and walked toward the truck, which had the logo of a fish painted on its side, with Arabic script beneath it.

"A refrigerated truck?"

"Yes. And this is not a real company." He pointed to the fish logo. "Do not stop for lunch or anything like this. You do not want Hezbollah or any of the Christian militias to become curious about you. The fuel tank is full."

"Okay," O'Hara replied.

"Do you want to have a swim in the pool, while I load the truck?"

"I'll just wait here." O'Hara wondered why the truck would not have been loaded and ready to go.

Vidic shrugged and walked into the garage. A moment later the door began to lower.

O'Hara walked over and sat on the stone ledge of the fountain, looking up at the few clouds that were stretched thin across the otherwise blue sky. He wondered what he might be delivering to Viktor that required refrigeration, and could not be pre-loaded.

A short while later, the garage door rose again and as it did, the truck ignition kicked on. Vidic climbed out of the driver's seat and beckoned for O'Hara to approach. "Remember, do not stop until you get to Jounieh."

"I'll drive straight there."

"Okay," Vidic said and clapped O'Hara on the back. "Next time you can fuck."

"Yeah," O'Hara said. He climbed up into the truck, and pulled the door shut. Arabic pop music was playing from the speakers on low volume. He pulled out of the garage and rolled down the window. "How do I get out?" he asked.

"It will open when you reach the gate."

O'Hara nodded and drove down the long, paved path.

He traveled the coastal road, focusing as much on the two side mirrors of the truck as on the road ahead, taking note of every make and color of vehicle that appeared behind him. He thought of the odd character Vidic and wondered whether the man knew how close he had come to having a gun drawn on him. The Glock had been with him since the Bronx, and it would have honored the men who had given it to him had they learned it was used to shoot a Serb. As he thought of those men, the memories felt so far removed from the place he now found himself that it was like being offered a glimpse into someone else's past.

* * *

The Bronx, New York — May 2020

The squat brick building west of Broadway was painted white and had protective grating over the windows that faced the sidewalk. There was no sign on the heavy steel front door that might suggest what existed beyond it. O'Hara banged on it with his fist and waited.

The door opened a few inches, revealing a slice of a young woman's masked face.

"Yes?" she asked.

"I'm here to see Agron," O'Hara responded.

"One moment." The woman closed the door and O'Hara could hear the slide of a bolt lock. A short while later he heard the sliding bolt once more and the door opened.

This time, standing at the door was a husky man in a polo shirt with curly black hair and deep-set hooded eyes the color of honeycomb. He wore a short cropped beard that had grayed in patches and when he smiled one of his side teeth was capped silver. He guided O'Hara inside and pulled the door closed behind him.

The office was decorated with cheap wood paneling with rows of gray filing cabinets pushed up against them. Cork boards hung on the wall over each of three desks, with thick collections of papers pinned to them. The woman who had answered the door was now sitting behind one of the desks, holding a phone to her ear. A red Albanian flag, with the black double-headed eagle at its center, hung on the back wall.

The man put an arm around O'Hara's shoulder and walked him toward a second door at the back of the room. "I'm Agron." He opened the door and called over his shoulder in Albanian to the woman behind the desk. O'Hara understood that he had told the woman not to interrupt them. He followed the man into a back room that smelled of stale tobacco smoke. A large flat-screen television hung on one wall and two leather couches lined the opposite side of the room. A green felt-lined gaming table was set in the middle, and was littered with folded newspapers.

Agron pulled out a pack of miniature cigars and offered one to O'Hara, who declined. He then stuck it in his own mouth. "Kreshnik said good things about you." The cigar bobbed between his lips as he spoke.

"He was very good to me."

The man lit the end of his cigar with a silver lighter and then snapped it shut. "He said he taught you how to speak?" Wisps of smoke escaped his mouth with his words.

"Just a few words here and there," O'Hara replied. "When you've got nothing but time, right?"

"Of course," Agron said. "Do you think he has a chance of getting out over the virus, also?"

O'Hara shrugged. "He was in there on a much heavier charge."

The man nodded. "Well even if he dies in there, it will still be worth what he did to that Serb." He tapped the end of his cigar against a glass tray.

"Some of the guys told me that story."

"Did they ever tell you what the Serbs did to his uncle in Kosovo?" Agron asked.

O'Hara shook his head.

"They are savages, cuz."

O'Hara nodded, unsure of what to say.

"So, as a favor to Kresh I can hire you as a painter. To satisfy any parole conditions. You won't ever have to show up to work."

"I'd appreciate that," O'Hara said.

Agron turned and opened a closet door where he crouched down before a large safe. He held his index finger against a sensor and the heavy metal door unlatched. He reached a hand in and pulled out a black pistol, and a small box of ammunition. He shut the safe door, and then walked over and lay the gun and box on the table.

"Glock 19. Kresh wanted you to have something with the chaos out there on the streets."

"Thank you."

Agron walked back to the closet and retrieved a duffel bag from an upper shelf. He picked up the gun and placed it in the bag along with the box of bullets and covered them with a few shirts that were embroidered

with his painting company's logo. He zipped the bag shut and handed it to
O'Hara, while guiding him out toward the front office.

* * *

Coast of Lebanon — July 2020

O'Hara made it south of Byblos before he felt comfortable to stop. He
turned onto an inland road that climbed the hills to an eventual lookout
with a small parking lot and a picturesque view of the coast below. He left
the truck's engine running, in case he needed to make a quick departure,
and climbed out of the driver's seat. He walked around back of the truck,
noticing that a padlock secured the rear door. Had he carried the right tools,
even a simple bobby pin, he could have had the lock picked in less than a
minute. He walked back to the front cab, and searched around behind the
seats for anything he might use to open it. There was a small tool box and a
crowbar tucked beneath the bench seating of the cab. He grabbed the
crowbar and carried it toward the rear of the truck.

He slid the forked end of the crowbar through the lock's ring and
twisted it until it snapped. He had done this many times before, with
shipping containers in Red Hook. There was a plastic band around one
handle, to show whether the truck had been opened prior to delivery.
O'Hara thought for a moment, and then unlatched the door, tearing the
band with it. He removed all traces of the band.

He turned the remaining lever that unlocked the reinforced door and
swung it open a crack. The darkness within prevented him from being able
to see anything at first. He opened the door a bit more, to allow a slice of
sunlight to enter the compartment. A small mound could be seen in the
middle of an otherwise empty space. O'Hara could not figure what it might
be from where he stood. He looked over his shoulder to see if any cars were
passing, before climbing up into the frigid bed of the truck. He fished his
cell phone from his pocket to use as a flashlight, and pulled the door closed
behind him.

As he drew near to the cargo, he used the beam of the flashlight to trace
the shape of the object, starting at one end, where he realized that the

cocoon-like outer layer was in fact a nylon sleeping bag. As he dragged his light from one end to the other, he froze. At the open end of the sleeping bag, he recognized a knit hat pulled down over loose strands of long, dark hair that lay sprawled in a mess along the floor of the truck bed.

His immediate thought was that he had been sent to transport a dead prostitute. He knelt down, and with one hand reached with two fingers to find the carotid artery in her neck. The body was still warm. Once he located the artery, he felt a faint thump of a pulse. He kept the light from his phone trained on her face as he rolled her body over. She appeared young, not yet a teenager, if he were to guess. Her face was doll-like, almost fake-looking. He pulled up the lid of one of her eyes and shined the light on a pinpoint pupil that did not dilate.

"Fuck," he said aloud, and stood. He walked back toward the door and climbed down from the truck bed, closing and latching the door shut. He then crossed the parking lot to the edge of the bluff and stared out toward the sea, trying to clear his mind enough to think.

He knew the obvious answer was to call Omar or Layla, but when he pulled the phone from his pocket he was overcome by an overwhelming wave of nausea. He leaned over the guardrail and vomited. There was the helpless feeling of having been ensnared by some sort of trap. As if he had traveled too deep down the rabbit hole to now find his way out. He had a strong urge to speak to the only person he might trust without consequence. He found Dina's number and dialed her.

"Hi," Dina said on the other end of the line.

"I need your help."

"Is everything okay?"

"Can we go to your place in Zahle a day early?"

"I work tonight."

"Can someone else cover your shift?"

"I suppose," she said, followed by a long pause. "What's wrong?"

"I'll tell you everything in person. Do you own a car?"

"Yes."

"Can you meet me somewhere north of Beirut?"

"Where?"

"Somewhere private. Anywhere. You know this country. I don't."

"I'm confused."

"Just pick a location somewhere between Beirut and Jounieh that is secluded and I'll meet you there. I'll explain everything."

"Um, okay? I will text you an address."

"Okay."

"It will take me about an hour to get there."

"Bring a padlock with you. Please."

"What?"

"A key lock. It doesn't matter what it looks like."

"I will have to buy one. Then it will take me longer to meet you."

"That's fine. See you there."

He hung up the phone and secured the latch in place to keep the door shut. When he received the text message from Dina, he went into his phone settings and turned on the GPS, and mapped the directions on how to get there. Then he climbed back into the truck and followed the route.

***

The trailhead parking lot was only large enough for four vehicles, and was enclosed on three sides by thickly wooded pine. The path that led in from the nearest road was long and winding, and O'Hara could hear sounds of tires crunching gravel for quite some time before Dina's vehicle came into view. She pulled up in a white Nissan SUV with tinted windows, and parked beside the box truck.

"What is going on?" she asked, getting out. She was smiling. "What is this truck?"

"I'm caught in the middle of something nasty," he said. "You're the only person I can trust."

"What is it?" she asked.

"I went and saw Viktor a couple days ago. He told me that I owed him a debt after fighting in his bar." O'Hara gestured over his shoulder at the truck. "He said I could clear the debt if I drive up and meet a Serbian guy in Monsef, where I would pick up this truck and then drive it to Jounieh to some property he owns."

"Property Viktor owns?"

O'Hara nodded.

"Who is the Serbian man?"

"Some guy, Vidic. Sound familiar? Maybe he's been to the bar." O'Hara ran his hand over his scalp. "Shaved head. Bent nose."

Dina shook her head. "I don't think so."

"I had a bad feeling about it all. Vidic made me wait outside while he loaded the truck inside his garage. Then he locked it shut and told me to drive straight to Jounieh without stopping. Something felt off, so I pulled over and snapped the lock on the door to see what was in the truck. Inside I found a body. A girl."

Dina gasped and looked around the parking lot, as though having forgotten that they were alone.

"I thought she was dead, at first. But I climbed in to have a closer look and found that she was breathing, but heavily drugged. She's just a kid."

"She's in there now?" Dina asked, with a horrified expression.

O'Hara nodded.

"There's no way I can deliver her to Viktor. I can't imagine what he would do with a young girl like that."

Dina ran her hand through her hair. "What do we do?"

"Can we take her to your place in Zahle until we figure out what to do with her? Would she be safe there?"

"Yes," Dina replied. "But then what? Viktor will look inside the truck and see she is missing."

O'Hara nodded. "Let me worry about that part. We need to figure out where she comes from and get her home. In the meantime she will have to be cared for as she goes through withdrawal from whatever drugs they've pumped into her."

She looked at the truck. "Can I see her?"

O'Hara unlatched the rear door and swung it open. He climbed up into the back and walked over and crouched down beside the sleeping girl. He slid his arms under her hips and shoulders and lifted her. "Easy, girl," he whispered, carrying her toward Dina, where he sat on the edge and slid off onto the gravel parking-lot floor.

"*Ya khusara,*" Dina said with a gasp.

Out in the daylight, O'Hara observed the girl's sleeping face. She had pale skin and black hair, and the cute nose and lips of a child. Seeing her this way, he believed her to be even younger than he had originally thought. He imagined the fear her parents must have felt at that very moment, wondering where she had gone and if she was even alive.

He carried the girl toward the Nissan. "Open the back door."

Dina rushed ahead of him and opened the door, and O'Hara laid the girl across the back seat. He felt her forehead, before closing the door.

"She doesn't look Lebanese," Dina said.

"Yeah, who knows," O'Hara said. "We can worry about that once she wakes up. Are you going to be okay with all of this?"

Dina nodded.

"Did you bring a lock?"

She opened the driver's side door of the Nissan, leaned in, and retrieved a new padlock and key, still encased in store-bought packaging.

"Perfect," he said, and tore open the plastic. He used the key to open the lock, then walked over to the rear door of the truck where he closed and latched the door shut, and locked it in place.

"Text me the Zahle address. I will meet you there, after I drop off the truck."

"How will you get there?"

"I'll find a way."

"And then what? When Viktor eventually opens the truck and finds it empty inside?"

"By then I'll have something figured out."

"I don't like this plan," Dina said.

He reached his hand up and touched the side of her face. "I will see you in Zahle." He then brought his head toward her until their foreheads touched. "Thank you for this." He kissed her.

CHAPTER EIGHT

Viktor lived in a large stone mansion on heavily wooded acreage outside Jounieh. A spire, poking out among the canopy of pines and cedars, was the only thing visible as O'Hara navigated the lone paved road that led to the property. O'Hara slowed the truck as he approached an iron gate. It opened electronically once he reached it. He then continued along the paved path that led toward an opulent stone structure of parapets and buttresses. He turned off the engine and climbed out of the truck.

The heavy timber doors beneath an arch-shaped entrance parted and Viktor emerged dressed in a t-shirt and red velour track pants. He was holding a pair of bolt cutters in one hand, and a cell phone pressed to his ear with the other. His clothes hung loosely from his gaunt frame, as he walked toward the truck, speaking in Russian to whoever was on the other side of the call. When he reached O'Hara he ended the call and slipped his phone into his pants pocket.

"What took you so long?" He seemed to stare through O'Hara, more than at him.

"You've got me driving around a country I've been in less than a week. Cut me some slack," O'Hara responded, using a confident tone to mask the fear he felt.

"Do you have a gun?"

O'Hara nodded.

"Put it on the front seat of the truck."

O'Hara pulled the Glock from the small of his back. Opened the driver's side door and set the pistol on the seat.

"Vidic thinks you are a strange man."

"The feeling is mutual."

"I don't understand this sentence you said," Viktor replied. "He told me you would not have any of his prostitutes."

"You should be happy I didn't. I would have taken even longer to get here."

Viktor's lip curled up into something between a grin and a snarl. He then walked toward the rear of the truck. O'Hara followed him.

Viktor inspected the padlock. "Where is the seal?" he asked.

"What seal?"

"The one that shows the door has not been opened."

"Viktor, I'm just the guy who drove it here. I have no clue what you're talking about."

"Did you open the truck?" Viktor asked.

"I know better than to do something like that." O'Hara waited for a response, but only received the Russian's ice cold stare. "No, I did not."

Viktor placed the teeth of the bolt cutters around the ring of the padlock, and squeezed the handles together, cutting through the metal. He handed the bolt cutters to O'Hara and removed the broken padlock from the door latch. He then pulled a stiletto knife from his pocket and used his thumb to engage a spring action blade, which shot forth from the handle. He pointed the long blade at O'Hara's face and held it that way for a moment before speaking.

"If there is anything wrong with this delivery, you will not be leaving this property."

Based only on his physical appearance, O'Hara would not have thought twice about meeting the man's threat with physical violence, but there was something in Viktor's sadistic eyes that caused O'Hara to trust the man's confidence.

"If there's anything wrong, you need to call your Serbian buddy," O'Hara said.

Viktor lowered the knife and held it at his side, as he used his other hand to free the latch and swing the door open. Viktor glanced at O'Hara, then pulled his cell phone out and shone its flashlight into the dark truck bed. He cursed in Russian.

Before Viktor could turn back toward him, O'Hara raised the bolt cutters and swung them hard across the back of the Russian's head, causing him to stumble against the truck bed and opening up a gash along his skull. The knife fell from his hand and landed on the grass. O'Hara hit him once more with the bolt cutters and pinned his body against the rear of the truck as he reached down and picked up the knife.

Viktor was conscious but disoriented, and tried wriggling free from where O'Hara had pinned him. O'Hara dropped the bolt cutters and used his free hand to push Viktor's face against the truck bed where he jammed the blade into the base of his skull, aiming to sever the brain stem. Viktor convulsed once, and went rigid. O'Hara held the blade in place until he felt the man's muscles relax, then twisted it. He looked over his shoulder at the mansion to make sure nobody else was present, before grabbing hold of the Russian's legs and lifting him up into the back of the truck, careful not to get blood on himself. He removed the knife from the back of Viktor's head, and retracted the blade. Blood began leaking more profusely from the wound, so he rolled the Russian's body further in, away from the edge. He then shut the door and secured the latch.

O'Hara walked over to the truck cab and tossed the switchblade onto the floorboard, near the passenger's seat. He wondered if there were surveillance cameras on the property, and assumed there were. He hoped that if so, they were not recording, as Viktor would not want any evidence of the girl having been delivered. He climbed into the truck, started the engine, and drove back out toward the main gate of the property.

Once back on the road, he pulled out his cell phone and dialed Omar's number.

* * *

Ouzai was a neighborhood near Rafic Hariri International airport, where every inch of decrepit or derelict buildings and shantytown alleys were painted in vibrant colors and covered with murals and artistic graffiti spray.

It was to O'Hara, as if someone took the concept of a 1980s New York City subway car, and applied it to an entire Beirut slum.

Omar was smoking a cigarette on a flat pad of rock that protruded from the sea behind a bright yellow and blue, windowless building. O'Hara climbed out of the driver's seat and met the Israeli at the rear of the truck.

Omar unlatched the rear door and opened it enough to peek inside before shutting it again. "How did this happen?"

An increasing roar thundered overhead as an airplane ascended into the sky above the slums, causing the ground to vibrate. As they waited for the noise to quiet, O'Hara studied the Israeli's face, wondering if he should have mentioned the girl.

"This was the truck I was told to pick up in Monsef. When I got to his property in Jounieh, he opened the back and pulled a knife on me." O'Hara nodded toward the rear doors of the truck. "I guess he was planning to kill me and stick me in there."

"The truck was empty?" Omar asked.

O'Hara nodded.

"All of this effort just to kill you?" Omar pulled hard on his cigarette and exhaled smoke with his words as he continued to speak. "He could have had you shot outside your flat in Beirut. Or kidnapped while walking home from Bar Sofia. He is *bratva*."

O'Hara shrugged. "Maybe it was a test?"

Omar clucked his tongue. "How did you prevent him from killing you?"

"I stuck a knife in his head."

Omar nodded. "And you are sure nobody was in his home who could have seen this?"

O'Hara shrugged, and waited to speak as another airplane soared overhead. "But that Serb knows I left with his truck to drive it to Viktor. Eventually people will begin to ask questions and he will mention me."

"I looked into this man. Radovan Vidic?"

"Unless there's more than one Vidic pimping hookers in Lebanon."

Omar nodded. "He is a known human trafficker. He brings girls in through Bulgaria and Turkey, down through Syria into Lebanon. I would assume that most of the prostitutes that show up to Bar Sofia were brought into the country by this man."

"Well, he'll pose a problem for me."

Omar nodded. "I will take care of him."

"How?"

Omar looked at him as he exhaled smoke from the side of his mouth. He dropped the cigarette to the ground and stubbed it out with his toe. "I handle a Hezbollah asset that would love to learn of this man's presence in Lebanon."

"Is it smart to involve people like Hezbollah?"

Omar shook his head. "Trust me. When they learn that he has purchased women from Islamic State across the border you will no longer have a problem."

"Islamic State?"

"It will sound better."

O'Hara frowned. "And what about this guy?" He gestured toward the truck.

"I will take care of him, myself," Omar said. "And the truck, too."

"What will you do with him?"

"He won't be the first person to disappear in south Beirut." Omar motioned toward the truck. "*Yalla*, I'll drive."

* * *

The microbus was crowded with four other passengers and smelled of stale tobacco smoke with hints of apple. The driver was a fat, sweaty man who talked with the passengers as if holding court, constantly gesturing with one hand while steering with the other. If O'Hara spoke Arabic he would have told the man to spend more time with his eyes on the road, and less looking at everyone in the rearview mirror. He sat alone in the back row and leaned his head against the window. He closed his eyes and allowed the unintelligible sounds of throaty Arabic to take on the effect of ambient noise. It was not long before he fell asleep.

He awoke when his body felt the vehicle come to a stop, and opened his eyes to find the fat driver turned in his seat, looking at him. "Zahle," the man said.

O'Hara leaned forward and fished a fistful of Lebanese notes from his pocket and handed them to the driver, assuming he had overpaid the man but wanting to avoid an argument that would create a scene where others in the street might later remember seeing his face. He stepped out of the microbus and called Dina.

He followed her directions up a hill past a church, some cafes, and a gun store until he found the roundabout Dina had described to him. From there he climbed another hill to a two-story home, set recessed among large boulders that shielded the property from the quiet, tree-lined road. As he made his way along a cobblestone driveway, he came to a set of slate stone steps where Dina was waiting at the front door of a stone cottage.

"How is she?" O'Hara asked.

Dina pursed her lips. "Very sick."

O'Hara climbed the stairs and kissed her. "She is going through withdrawals."

"How long does it last?"

He shrugged. "Can't last forever. Just keep giving her water. We don't want her dehydrating with all the vomiting and diarrhea."

Dina led him through the front door and closed it behind him.

Inside were rooms of exposed stone walls and dark wooden floorboards. Timber rafters ran the length of the ceiling, forming grid-like patterns. He followed her down a hall lined with photographs of Paris on one side, into an open kitchen and dining room. The counters and sink were stainless steel and the kitchen cabinets matched the color of the floorboards.

"Do you want to see her? She was sleeping when I last checked."

"Let her sleep. I'll see her when she wakes."

Dina pointed to a steel percolator that rested on the stovetop. "I brewed coffee when you called."

"Good idea." O'Hara walked over to her while she poured coffee into a mug and handed it to him. "Thanks." He drank some. "Do we know her name?"

Dina shook her head. "She has only screamed and cried, and vomited. I do not think she understands anything I have said to her. Arabic, English or French."

O'Hara shook his head.

"There are organizations that handle situations like this," Dina said.

"Yeah, but everyone out here seems to answer to someone else. We need to be careful who we trust."

He had been on the verge of telling Omar about the girl since Ouzai, but the fact that the Israeli had admitted to handling a contact among Hezbollah, the same organization that invited Russian mercenaries to operate in Lebanon, gave the whole situation enough of an incestuous feel to dissuade him from doing so. If he had made a mistake by allowing Omar to take the truck with Viktor's body, only he would suffer the repercussions. He couldn't bear the idea of making a mistake with the girl's life.

"We don't want to be accused of kidnapping."

O'Hara nodded. "You're right."

They heard a loud, muffled groan through the ceiling.

O'Hara sighed. "Let's just figure out who she is, first."

Dina placed a hand on the side of his face and frowned in what seemed to be an expression of empathy. She gestured through an open doorway toward a lounge room that was filled with velvet-cushioned sofas. "Come."

She led him into the lounge and sat on the longest of the sofas, beneath an intricately carved wood sculpture of a Lebanese flag. She patted the cushion beside her.

"What happened with Viktor?" she asked, once he was seated.

He didn't answer. She rested her coffee on one of the terra-cotta end tables and shifted position so that she was behind him. She placed her hands on either side of his neck and began massaging the muscles of his shoulders.

"You're so tense," she said, and pulled him back so that he was leaning against her. "Relax." She move her hands to his forehead, where she began rubbing small circles against his brows. O'Hara felt a release from within, as if he had submitted something of himself to her. His vision blurred as tears welled up in his eyes.

"You are safe with me," she whispered, as if able to read his emotions.

O'Hara remained silent. He did not understand what was happening, but knew it was something that Dina had unlocked from within him. Something he had been carrying with him for ages. She moved her hands from his brow, to the top of his head, and caressed him like a mother might a grieving child. In those moments, O'Hara felt something that he had not felt from another person in as far back as his memory allowed. He knew that he needed to be honest with her, about everything.

He didn't have the courage to face her so he spoke with the back of his head resting against her breast. "There are things I need to tell you. Things that might cause you to want me to leave this house and never speak to you again." He used the collar of his shirt to dab at his eye. "But I can't lie to you anymore."

Dina's hands went still as he said this.

"Nothing you know about me is true." He took a deep breath before continuing. "My name isn't Donovan Burke. It's O'Hara Poit. I'm from New York, not Boston. Less than two months ago I was sitting in prison, serving a sentence for the burglary of a small museum. One day I was unexpectedly released because of what I was told was an outbreak of Covid among the prisoners. First day out of prison I was introduced to some people who offered me a lot of money to travel west with them, to the state of Idaho."

O'Hara allowed Dina a chance to respond, but she said nothing.

"In Idaho, I was introduced to a man who ran a large community of right-wing separatists. Conservative types... that believe America is under threat from corruption within their own government. I came to find out that this man was politically connected, and directly played a role in my having been released from prison. It was explained to me that the real reason I was set free and tempted to Idaho with offers of money was because my best friend from childhood, a man named Jared Ingleton, was involved with a violent militant movement being trained by Russian mercenaries here in Lebanon. I was told that after their training was complete, my friend's group would return to the United States to commit violence in the streets of America."

Dina cleared her throat. "Is Jared one of the men who come to Bar Sofia?"

"Yes." He paused to give her a chance to speak, before continuing. "In Idaho I was given a new identity and a passport. I was sent here to make contact with him."

"How does Layla fit into your story? You said you knew her before coming here."

"She works for a group of people that helped me enter the country."

Dina's hands stopped caressing him when he said this.

For a while, they were both silent.

"I'm in over my head at this point," he said finally.

"What does this sentence mean?"

"When I dropped the truck off to Viktor today, he opened the back and saw there was nothing inside. He pulled a knife on me."

"And yet, you are here," she said.

"I am," O'Hara repeated.

"I see," she said.

He felt the rise of her chest against the back of his head as she breathed in. Then she exhaled, slowly. "My uncle was a gangster in Beirut, you know. Many years ago. My mother's brother. He was murdered during the war years, before I was born. But it is because of his reputation that Ali offered me the job to work at Bar Sofia. And it is because of him that I am not treated disrespectfully, like the other women that have worked there."

O'Hara remained silent.

"My parents always taught me that my uncle was a good man, despite his reputation. This is Lebanon, *ya hayati*. Life is not black and white here. To persevere we live in the gray. Sometimes good men have to do bad things." She kissed the top of his head. "Thank you for being honest with me."

O'Hara nodded and bit down hard on his lip.

Dina wrapped her arms around his shoulders and hugged him, resting her chin on his head.

***

The girl was retching when O'Hara and Dina entered the room. Curled up in a fetal position on the bed, she looked as though she had not slept in ages. O'Hara helped her sip from a mug of hot tea, while Dina used a wet rag to wash her face and neck.

"What is your name?" O'Hara asked her, in English.

"Valmira," the girl said, in a scratchy whisper. "Me, no English."

O'Hara looked at Dina. "What kind of name is that?"

Dina shrugged. "Where are you from?"

The girl did not respond. She lay back against her pillow and mumbled something in what sounded like a pleading tone. O'Hara was shocked to find that he recognized a few words.

"*Shqip*?" he asked her, using the Albanian name for the language.

She looked up at him and used his arm to pull herself back up into a sitting position. "You are Albanian?" she asked him back, in her language.

He shook his head. "I know words," he said, using hand gestures to help convey his message. "A little."

The girl began to cry and leaned her forehead against his shoulder. He held her, and caressed her head. Dina took the tea from him and helped her sip.

"What are you speaking?" Dina asked.

"She's Albanian," he said.

"You speak Albanian?"

"No. I can just string together a few words here and there, to get a point across. I used to hang out with a lot of Albanians."

"You are safe, now," O'Hara said to the girl in English, and touched her shoulder. He tried to remember some of the words he had once grown used to hearing among the inmates. "Tell me. You. From where."

"Vlore," she responded, and motioned for more tea.

Dina helped her drink from the mug.

"Vlore is in Albania?" O'Hara asked.

She nodded. "Who are you?"

"Donovan," he said and touched his chest. He frowned, unable to remember the words to explain more. He moved a strand of hair from her face. "How many years? You. Valmira."

"Twelve."

O'Hara shook his head and translated her age for Dina.

"Where am I?"

"Lebanon."

Valmira began to sob. "Where is Lebanon?" she asked.

"A country."

She put her hands over her ears, as if reliving a memory in real time, and said something unintelligible in rapid Albanian.

O'Hara caressed her arm. He turned and relayed everything to Dina, who then shifted to the other side of Valmira and wrapped her arms around her in a hug.

"You have father? Name?"

She wiped tears from her eyes with her palms. "His name is Besart Duka."

"Besart Duka," O'Hara repeated. He walked over to a bedside table and retrieved a pen and paper and handed it to Valmira. "Besart Duka," he said, gesturing for her to write the name down, which she did.

O'Hara turned to Dina. "Do you have a laptop or something we can use to try and track down her father?"

"Downstairs," Dina said, with a nod of her head.

CHAPTER NINE

All it took was O'Hara typing her father's name into a search engine on Dina's laptop to realize what kind of man they would be dealing with. There were only a few English language results, but once clicked, each of the links brought him to news articles discussing organized crime in the Balkans and across the Adriatic Sea in Bari, Italy. There was nothing about her disappearance.

O'Hara wrote down the name of a hotel that one article claimed Besart had ties to, and typed it into the search engine. The results showed multiple photos of beautiful beaches that looked more like a Caribbean setting than what O'Hara imagined Albania would look like. Below those, an address in a town called Himare, along with a phone number, was listed. O'Hara wrote down the information and shut the laptop.

He pulled out his cell phone and dialed the hotel's phone number. After a few rings, a woman answered the phone. O'Hara explained that he spoke only English, and asked to speak to Besart Duka. The woman on the phone, who spoke perfect English, stated that there was no guest by that name staying in the hotel. O'Hara then told her that he had information about Valmira Duka, and would call back in thirty minutes. He disconnected the call before she could respond.

Dina was upstairs helping Valmira to bathe, so he walked over and poured himself a fresh coffee and waited. When thirty minutes had passed, he dialed the hotel's number once more. The woman answered on the first ring. O'Hara confirmed that he had called earlier, when a man's voice suddenly came on the line.

"Who are you?!" the man demanded in accented English.

"Is this Besart?"

"Where is my daughter?!"

"She is safe. I'm calling to get her back to you."

"Tell me your name!"

"Donovan."

"Where are you?!"

"Lebanon."

"Lebanon!?"

"I believe she was kidnapped and brought here. I discovered her by accident."

"She was stolen off the street in Albania. Now are you telling me she is in Lebanon?!"

"I don't know the details. Just know that she is now safe. You don't have to worry any longer, you just have to help me organize a way to get her to you. I will tell you everything I know once we meet in person. I don't want to say any more over the phone."

"I must speak to her."

"One moment."

O'Hara brought his phone upstairs and knocked on the door. Dina let him inside, where Valmira was sitting on the bed, wrapped in a duvet and nursing a cup of hot tea. He handed her the phone. "Your father."

"Papa!" she shouted into the phone. She spoke in Albanian and began to cry, nodding her head, listening for a long time without speaking. "Okay, Papa." She held the phone back out to O'Hara, who took hold of it.

"Hello," O'Hara said. He exited the bedroom and pulled the door shut behind him.

"Who are the men that had her when you found her?"

"I promise to tell you everything in person."

"This must be kept a secret until she is with me. There are reasons I have not gone to the police about her disappearance."

"I will tell nobody. I don't trust anyone in this country."

"Can you keep her safe until tomorrow night? I will have to find a way past the travel restrictions."

"I can keep her safe for as long as you need me to."

"Where will I meet you?"

"Take down my number."

O'Hara told Besart his mobile phone number. "Call that number when you land in Beirut and I will have a place we can meet."

"If this a trap you will not survive."

"It's no trap. I'm sure people will want me dead for taking your daughter from them."

"It will be them who die," Besart said. "If you are not deceiving me, you will be rewarded for this."

"I just want her back with her family."

"Thank you."

"See you tomorrow," O'Hara said, and ended the call.

Not long after, Dina came downstairs holding a wet cloth, which she walked over and threw into a washing machine. "She is finally sleeping," she said.

"She needs it," he said.

"Are you hungry?"

"I could eat," he replied.

"I'll go to the grocer and butcher, and will cook us a meal. I can make a soup for Valmira."

O'Hara pulled a thick roll of American dollars from his pocket and handed them to her. "You can use this, right?"

"It is actually better, these days." She reached up and touched the side of his face, and waited for him to look at her before speaking. "You are a good man," she said.

He nodded, but said nothing.

"You did the right thing."

"Thank you."

"A man once did things to me, when I was not much older than Valmira."

"What do you mean?"

She ran her finger along the scar beneath her jawline. "Not far from here. He pressed a knife into my neck."

O'Hara reached out and held her. "Dealing with Valmira must stir... up so many emotions in you."

Dina shook her head, and offered a slight smile. "It is okay, it was long ago. But this is the real reason my parents live in France."

"I don't follow," O'Hara said.

"My father hunted down the man."

"He had to flee the country?"

"We left before it could become an issue." She shrugged. "It is why I did not return to Lebanon until university. Like I told you, we live in the gray, here." She leaned in and kissed him on the lips. "Everyone in this country has secrets they do not share." She turned and left the house.

Once she had gone, O'Hara walked into the lounge room and lay down on the couch. He had been running on caffeine and adrenaline since meeting Vidic that morning. It was hard to believe it was still the same day, when he thought back on all that had occurred. He thought of Besart Duka, empathizing with the man while trying to imagine the inner turmoil he must have suffered while not knowing where his little girl had disappeared to, or if she were even alive. He wondered if he would have trouble entering Lebanon on such short notice. Before he could come up with an answer to that question, he fell asleep.

***

He awoke to the sounds of Dina entering the front door, carrying two paper bags of groceries. She rested them on the kitchen counter and began removing items, laying the ingredients out along an island counter in the middle of the room. Bottles of red wine and olive oil. Chicken breasts. Eggplant. Garlic.

"Can I help with anything?" O'Hara asked.

"No, *ya hayati*, this is my treat for you." She gestured toward the wine bottles. "You can open a bottle and pour us both a glass. The corkscrew should be in that drawer."

O'Hara opened the drawer and found it. He pulled the cork from a bottle and filled two glasses that Dina had removed from an overhead cabinet. He handed one to her, and slid onto a stool at the kitchen counter, watching as she began slicing the eggplant. She was smiling.

His nerves were wrecked and her mood confused him.

"What's got you so happy?" O'Hara asked.

"This reminds me of how my mother would cook for my father when I was a child. When he returned from conferences or meetings in Beirut, and would walk through that door." She gestured toward the front entrance. "Always with his necktie loosened and the top few buttons of his shirt undone. And they would drink wine together, and eat, and he would read me poems by Hafez."

Imagining her happy family caused O'Hara to smile. It was something he had no ability to relate to. Other than the brief period of his teenage years, while living with Red and Nan in Queens, he did not have a single memory of having ever been cooked for. He could not remember a time where his two parents had ever shared the same room long enough to eat a meal, and was unsure that they ever had.

Dina began mincing garlic and mixing it into a batch of thick yogurt with a wisp. When her glass ran low O'Hara refilled it from the bottle. He then topped off his own glass.

"Were you surprised to recognize that Valmira was speaking Albanian?"

"Hell, yeah. I spent a lot of time with Albanians in prison. They liked to talk to one another in their language so that the other inmates wouldn't understand what they were saying."

"And that's how you learned?"

O'Hara shook his head. "Like I said, I only know a handful of words."

"Isn't it interesting how it was the one language we needed and you had it? That could have even been the real purpose of you having gone to prison. To rescue Valmira. It could have been an important part of your contractual path."

"I can think of more pleasant ways to learn some Albanian." He sipped his wine.

Dina laughed and walked to the sink to wash her hands before drying them with a dish towel. She picked up her wine glass and walked over and sat on his leg, draping her free arm around his shoulder. "I can feel in my heart that there have been many things drawing you to be in Lebanon right now. This was obviously one of those things."

O'Hara didn't speak. He was staring past her lap, toward the floor, pondering the possibility.

"It is important that you have compassion for yourself, and forgive yourself for anything that occurred. Remind yourself that it all resulted in you saving this innocent girl's life."

O'Hara looked up at her.

"That is all in the past, O'Hara. Just be here now. The present. In love and gratitude."

"That sounds easier said than done in this crazy world."

"They cannot be forced emotions. It will happen naturally, once you strip away the fears and attachments."

Unsure of what exactly she was talking about, he slid his arm behind her waist and hugged her. "You are a special person."

She smiled. "Remember. In love and gratitude."

He rested his head against her chest. "In love," he said.

She kissed the top of his head.

* * *

O'Hara couldn't remember the last time he had eaten such a meal. His stomach was full and his head was feeling warm and fuzzy from the wine. He stood belly-up to the sink, rinsing plates and loading them onto a drying rack. Dina was wiping down the countertops with a kitchen towel, and humming along with the classical music that streamed from a website on her laptop.

Valmira had yet to wake, and when Dina had gone upstairs to check on her shortly after dinner, she was snoring among the duvets, a messed head of black hair barely visible. They did not bother to wake her to eat the soup Dina had prepared.

As they were finishing cleaning up, the power went out. Dina suggested they open another bottle of wine and take it out on the terrace that overlooked the slope of a rocky hillside at the back of the property. Under the crisp canopy of shimmering constellations, among the strong scent of mountain pines, O'Hara leaned against the iron guardrail and stared up into the night, in awe of the low dusting of stars. Since Dina was the only one to ever use the Zahle property, and rarely did so, the patio contained no outdoor furniture. She went upstairs and returned with three large blankets and spread them out on the terrace floor. They sat on the blankets, and O'Hara filled their glasses with wine from the newly opened bottle.

"I wish I could live here, just doing this every night."

Dina smiled. "And how would you support yourself?"

O'Hara looked over, noticing her eyelids were heavy. He wasn't sure if it was because of the wine, or feeling tired, or both, but it gave her a seductive look that made him want to lie down with her on the blankets. "Maybe you and I could crack into the wine industry."

"What do you know about the wine industry?" she asked, playfully.

O'Hara sipped from his glass. "I know how to keep it in business."

Dina laughed, and leaned into him, resting her head on his shoulder. Together, they looked up at the sky. Two stars streaked across the darkness, in different directions, leaving an imprinted trail behind them.

"Beautiful," she whispered.

"Did you make a wish?"

She nodded.

O'Hara spotted another slow-moving star, traveling westward. He pointed at it. "Check that out," he said. "Satellite?"

"Maybe not," she said.

As if responding to her words, the object hooked a turn and shot across the sky at a speed far faster than the stars had streaked. Then it vanished.

"Holy shit!" O'Hara gasped. He looked at Dina, who was grinning. She did not look anywhere near as surprised as he felt.

"Was that your wish?" he asked.

"No, but it might have been yours."

"What did you wish for?" he asked.

With that, she turned him by the shoulders and laid back on the blankets, pulling him with her. He allowed himself to be drawn down on top of her and leaned his head so that their lips met. He had no way of realizing how special it was that she chose him, but he sensed it. He wondered if she knew that his own wish was about to come true.

CHAPTER TEN

Valmira was sitting on the couch in the lounge room with a blanket draped over her shoulders, being fed spoonfuls of the soup Dina had prepared the night before. Color had returned to her face although she was still withdrawn.

Dina had spoken little of what occurred the previous night, but smiled every time she met eyes with O'Hara, who was busy cooking breakfast for the two of them. The rich aroma of brewed Yemeni coffee filled the ground floor of the house, and through the open windows roosters could be heard crowing in the distance.

O'Hara carried in two plates of scrambled eggs and buttered slices of French baguette, and set them down on the table before Dina.

"She seems to be taking to the soup," he said.

"Yes," she answered. "Thank you for breakfast." She picked up a fork and stabbed at some of the eggs.

"You've been quiet today," O'Hara said.

Dina smiled and chewed her food.

"Is everything okay?"

Dina nodded and fed another spoonful of soup to Valmira.

"You are the first person I have done that with," she said. "Since this." She touched her finger to the scar on her neck.

He kissed two of his fingers and touched them to her scar. "You can release that."

"You have all of me now," she said, softly.

"That's all I need," he answered.

She smiled.

"You dreamed, last night," he said. "I thought you were having a seizure."

Dina nodded.

"Are they always that intense?"

She nodded once more.

"What was this one about?"

"She led me through a forest, to an old man who was sitting around a campfire. I believe it was Australia. He was dark-skinned, with long woolly gray hair and a beard, and with dots painted all over his face."

"Sounds like those Aborigines."

She nodded. "Exactly. There was a clearing in the canopy above the fire, so that we could see all the stars and planets, through the tree tops." She pointed upward with her finger. "I have never encountered this man in previous dreams, but I felt as though I already knew him. And I knew somehow that he was a keeper of wisdom. As if he had knowledge about the universe, something like this." She lifted her mug and took a sip of coffee. "He did not speak. We were communicating through thoughts. Telepathic." She set her mug back down on the table. "He told me that I am on a journey that doesn't end here, in Lebanon. But that I must end up in the land of his people. It is where I will fully harness my gift of dreaming." She pointed out the window, toward the sky. "I know it sounds crazy."

O'Hara shook his head. "Nothing sounds crazy after the month I've just lived."

She smiled.

"I guess we are headed to Australia, then."

"You do believe me, don't you?" she asked, sounding almost skeptical.

"Yes." He looked at Valmira, who was watching them, unable to understand anything that was being said.

Just then his cell phone rang. He walked over to where it lay on the kitchen counter and held it to his ear.

"Hello," he said.

"Aye," Red's deep voice replied. "It's me."

"Where're you at?" O'Hara asked.

"Can you make it to Baalbek?"

"Stand by," O'Hara said, and covered the mouthpiece of the phone. "How far is Baalbek from here?"

"About forty minutes, if you drive," Dina said. "Microbus will take a little longer with stops."

"Yeah, I can get there," he said into the phone. "It'll take about an hour."

"I have to be back at the camp in about two hours."

"Alright, I'll leave now. Are you alone?"

"I will be, while most of these cats go to Friday mosque. But there's always the risk of bumping into someone."

"Where's a good spot we can meet to keep that risk low?"

"You know how to get to the Roman ruins?"

"I'll find 'em."

"That's our best shot at spotting surveillance."

"I'll leave here in about ten."

"I'll be there."

O'Hara hung up and turned to Dina.

She reached up and touched the side of his face, then gave an understanding nod.

He leaned down and kissed her.

* * *

As he traveled the main thoroughfare into Baalbek, the paved boulevard seemed to divide two worlds. To his right was a crowded village of squat buildings where dense blocks were separated by narrow alleyways, giving it the appearance of one large bazaar. Down each alley he passed, shops sold a variety of wares from rugs to metalwork, to Hezbollah-themed shirts. Opposite the town, O'Hara could already see the high, stone columns of an ancient ruin that stood tall against a clear blue sky. As he drew closer he passed beneath an endless line of yellow and green Hezbollah flags, which hung from light posts beside framed posters of martyrs that had lost their lives for the party's cause.

O'Hara followed signs that were written in Arabic and English, indicating where the turnoff for the ruins was located. He pulled off the main road and into a gravel lot, where few vehicles were parked. He locked Dina's car and followed a walkway to a gate, where he paid a fee to an elderly man wearing a head wrap, and entered into one of the most well-preserved Roman sites on earth.

It was like passing through a portal and stepping into a post-apocalyptic battleground of ancient gods. The place was surrounded by towering columns and stone structures adorned with intricately sculpted animal statues and other depictions of antiquity.

It was not hard for him to spot the lone black man on the grounds. Red wore tactical style sunglasses and a sand-colored ball cap. He was sitting along the edge of a stone cliff, staring out over the rolling hill towns of the Bekaa Valley.

O'Hara climbed a chiseled staircase up to the base of the gargantuan columns and walked up behind his old friend. He sat down beside him on the edge of the cliff, allowing his feet to hang over the hundred foot drop to the earth below. He glanced over at Red, who continued to stare off into the distance.

"Lebanon Red," O'Hara said.

Red looked over. There was no warmth in his expression. "What are you doing in Lebanon? And what the fuck was that all about in Beirut?"

"No, this starts with me asking the questions." O'Hara cleared his throat and spit off the edge. "Are you the reason I went to prison?"

"What?!" Red asked, as if offended by the question.

"I was told you're the snitch that got me put away?"

"Fuck you," Red responded. "My grandmother raised you. You think I'd sell you out?"

"I saw government documents that state you did. That you got rolled up for selling steroids and turned informant to save your own ass."

"Wait, what?"

"You heard me."

"I got banged for juice, and cut a deal with the government." Red nodded as he said this. "But it had nothing to do with you."

"Explain, then."

"Nah, fuck that." Red shifted his body away from O'Hara so that he was beyond his reach. "You're telling me you saw government papers that claim I cooperated against you? Who showed that to you, because I guarantee that fucking thing was forged."

O'Hara did not respond. He thought back to the document he was shown in Idaho. Staring at his old friend, his childhood brother, brought back a flood of emotions and disarmed him in a way he wasn't prepared for. He wanted to hear that Red had never betrayed him. But, he knew that if that were the case, it would force him to have to question every single fact that he had believed to be true since his release from prison. He leaned back on his elbows and looked up at the sky.

"Where did you disappear to while I was locked up? After my first year inside, the letters stopped."

"That's around when I got bagged for bringing the juice in from Mexico. That's what I'm saying, bro. You were already locked up by then."

O'Hara studied his eyes. If he were telling the truth, it meant the dates on Senator Tade's document were falsified. "And when Nan passed? Why wasn't I told?"

He noticed a visible change in Red's expression. His lip twitched and for a moment it looked as though he might tear up.

Red exhaled slowly. "Bro, that was the worst part about all of it. I was in the Feds serving a six-month stretch when she passed. They didn't even let me bury her."

O'Hara stared out across the valley.

"I wasn't able to get her a headstone until I was out."

"I visited her."

"You did," Red said, then nodded.

"She'd be happy with the stone you chose." O'Hara placed a hand on Red's shoulder. "Why are you out here, bro?"

Red inhaled deeply, then sighed. "Some government cats came to me when I was in Allenwood. They offered me a deal where I'd be done with time already served, if I agreed to go deep into this militia."

"The American government sent you out here?"

Red shook his head. "Nah, they had me up in the militia long before any of this talk of coming overseas started up. I was in with these dudes, posted up in a couple spots. Detroit. Baltimore. Brooklyn. I worked my way up to running a crew of my own. Then a couple years in, they started meeting with some Russians and arranged for some of us to come out here and be trained in military tactics and guerrilla warfare by some bad motherfuckers. Spetznaz type shit."

"What's the end goal?" O'Hara asked. He wanted to see how much of what he had been told in Idaho was true. "What happens once you guys are trained up?"

"We are supposed to go back home and fuck shit up."

"So do you buy into all this black nationalist shit? Or are you just a mole?"

"O'Hara, what's wrong with you? The only brother I ever had in this life is white. The only other person my Nan looked after and loved as much as she loved me..." Red paused for a moment, as if lost in thought, "was white. There's a lot of fucked up racism going on back there. But, you and I were never like that, bro."

"Who's your handler, then?"

"Nah, hang on." Red pointed at O'Hara. "I just came clean to you. Your turn."

O'Hara had no fact-based reason to believe Red was being any more truthful than anyone else had been up until this point. But in his gut, he already knew that he believed his old friend.

"I was released almost two months ago. Some lawyer showed up and told me it was due to the pandemic and an outbreak among inmates. That since I had served a good chunk of my time and had no major issues inside, they were letting me out. So that first night, I go downtown to that joint we used to go to, under the donut shop. It was still operating on the low, despite the social restrictions and all that."

A slight smile appeared on Red's face as he remembered the place.

"Inside I met these dudes who were there hanging out, in town from Idaho. We hit it off over a few rounds of beers. Said they ran some off-the-grid community back there, preppers and libertarians and shit. By last call, they had made me an offer that was worth dipping out on my parole for. So a few days later, I end up driving cross-country with them to Idaho to what turned out to be a big-ass separatist community." He gestured toward Red. "The guys that are standing across the arena from the group you're rolling with, expecting a civil war down the line. So I end up living in this community for a stretch, and eventually come to learn that they're tied in with some heavy politicians in DC, and that it was these Idaho folks who were behind me being released from prison, all along."

"How would they pull that off? Why?"

O'Hara pointed a finger at Red. "They knew all about you and your crew. And they knew about how tight you and I were."

"But I'm in this shit on behalf of the American government."

"That's the weird part," O'Hara said. "To be honest, I don't think they know that."

"And you said they're a separatist group? Who're the politicians they're in bed with?"

"I only met one. Some Idaho senator called Tade. There are others, though. Some Israelis, too."

"Israelis?" Red asked. "So hold up. You were released from prison to come out here and get in contact with me, and then do what?"

"Persuade you to be a source of information. Basically do what you're telling me you already do for someone else."

"The damn Feds, is who." Red shook his head. "You've been played, bro."

O'Hara nodded. "Maybe."

"Now what?"

"I'll need some time to wrap my head around it all."

Red glanced at him out of the corner of his eye.

"O'Hara, I wouldn't have risked my ass to come and meet you in secret if I was gonna just lie to you." He thumbed his finger over his shoulder. "If any of them Russians caught us talking here. Me, with the reason I'm out here, and you being some shady American that just broke my man's jaw. It would be bullets in our heads."

"When are you guys due to head back to America?"

"Not sure. It's sounding like it could be weeks, days even. We're trained up and ready."

"If you're in a leadership position, how do you not know when you'll be leaving?"

"That info is all compartmentalized. I get the scoop at the last minute, always."

"Will you head back down to Beirut for a night out before you go?"

Red shrugged.

"Keep my phone number. If anything crazy is coming, find a way to call me."

Red nodded, and climbed to his feet. O'Hara did the same.

"I missed you, bro," Red said. "It was the hardest part of going deep. Never having the chance to explain anything."

O'Hara slapped hands with him, and they pulled one another in for a tight hug.

"We got caught up," O'Hara said. He thumped Red's back with an open hand. "Even if we had to come to this insane part of the world to make it happen."

Red grinned, and released his hug. He held up a fist between them, and O'Hara knocked knuckles with him. "I'll be in touch."

O'Hara nodded and watched as his friend turned and disappeared down the stone steps.

CHAPTER ELEVEN

O'Hara's cell phone chimed and a text message from Omar appeared on the screen. It read, 'turn on the news.'

"Is there a way to watch the local news, here?" he asked Dina.

She pulled her own cell phone from her pocket, and began tapping her finger on the screen. She then handed it to him.

O'Hara watched the screen, as a man's voice narrated in Arabic over footage of a location he immediately recognized. The video cut to show men dressed in olive green military fatigues escorting a beaten, bloodied and handcuffed Vidic past the statue outside his home, and forcing him into the back of a windowless van before slamming the door shut. The broadcast cut to a video of a bookish, bearded man wearing thick-framed glasses and a head wrap, who spoke Arabic directly toward the camera.

"Who's this guy and what's he saying?" O'Hara asked Dina, and handed her back the phone.

"Nasrallah," she said. "The leader of Hezbollah. He is saying that his men have captured a human trafficker in Lebanon that was managing a major prostitution ring in the country." Her eyes widened and she looked at him, then at Valmira. "He also says that Hezbollah has taken the matter into their own hands because of the worthless Lebanese government, who allowed this disease to continue to spread within our country. He says, Hezbollah always protects the Lebanese people and has removed this cancer, thanks be to Allah."

"That's the Serb," O'Hara said to Dina, with a slight nod of his head toward Valmira.

Just then, O'Hara's phone rang. He held up a finger to Dina, and answered it.

"Hello?" he said.

"It is Besart," the voice answered. "I have crossed into northern Lebanon. I am near Tripoli."

"I thought you were going to call me from the Beirut airport."

"I flew to Turkey. Air travel into Lebanon is too complicated. Where do I meet you?"

"Are you alone?"

"No."

"How many people are with you?"

"Me and two others."

O'Hara had already chosen a place to meet the man. A place where, he figured, he would have the best chance of not getting them all killed while he vetted Besart and his intentions.

"I will meet you inside the Mohammed al-Amin mosque, in Beirut." Knowing that many Albanians were Muslims, he was hoping Besart wouldn't attempt any acts of violence in a place of worship.

"When?" Besart asked.

"Say two hours."

"I will be there," Besart said, and ended the call.

* * *

The crowd had thinned out, with the Friday services having finished hours earlier. O'Hara handed his shoes to a man dressed in a *gallibeya* robe, who had a soot-stained callous on his forehead from countless contacts with coarse prayer mats, multiple times a day. The man stuck the shoes in a cubbyhole, alongside multiple other pairs, and welcomed O'Hara into the mosque with a sweeping hand and a slight bow.

O'Hara made his way over to a marble column and sat on the carpeted floor, on which rows of intricately stitched designs indicated the direction one should face when communing with Allah. He rested his back against the column and kept his attention focused on the front entrance of the mosque, while pretending to observe the hanging chandeliers and painted arched domes above. He respected the devotion of Muslims, who never seemed to waver when it came to having faith in what they believed. He took the opportunity to ask that Allah and any other divinity that might have been listening in that moment, would allow nothing bad to occur during his meeting with Besart.

When the Albanian walked in, wearing a black-collared shirt and jeans, O'Hara recognized him from a few photographs found on the internet. He was a barrel-chested man, below average height with thick arms. His short-cropped, receding hair, and the slight dusting of a beard were peppered with shades of gray. The Albanian scanned the room before walking to a spot on the carpet and standing with his eyes closed. He held his arms out before him with palms upturned, then folded one across the other, over his stomach. He dropped to his knees where he completed the prostrations of the Muslim prayer sequence.

A few moments after Besart entered, two more men came in. The first was a skinny man with parted hair and a beak-like nose, whose thick Adam's apple was so pronounced that it made his neck appear bent. The second man appeared slightly younger, and was powerfully built — like a man who had spent a lifetime shoveling concrete or laying cinderblock. They both wore t-shirts and jeans, and O'Hara could see tattoo ink poking out from under their sleeves. They stayed close to one another and took up prayer stations on the carpet, a half-dozen rows behind where Besart now knelt.

Once O'Hara was sure Besart had finished praying, he stood and approached him. He noticed the two men at the back watching him as he walked, and gave a slight nod of acknowledgement before taking a seat on the carpet.

"Donovan," Besart asked, without looking at him.

"I recognized you from the internet."

"Do not believe everything that is written about me on the internet."

"Your life is your own business."

"Did you choose to meet in a mosque because you knew I was Muslim?"

"Yes."

"And you thought no harm will come to you, because of this?"

"I thought it was less likely."

"You have nothing to fear from me, if you are honest with me and bring me my daughter."

"You will have your daughter, today. She is safe."

"Where is she?"

"She is being looked after by my girlfriend, about ninety-minutes drive from here. Nobody else knows where she is."

"Take me there."

"I can't. If you rent a hotel room I'll bring her to you."

"I have rented a suite, already. I won't leave Beirut until I figure out who took her."

"I know two men that were involved. But I do not know enough of the details to figure out the whole story."

"What were their names?"

"We can talk more when I meet you with Valmira."

"If everything you tell me is true, then I will owe you a debt."

"You will not." O'Hara cleared his throat. "It sickens me, what occurred."

A long silence followed. Besart then turned his head and extended his hand, which O'Hara clasped. "You will be like blood to me, once I have her."

O'Hara nodded.

"Okay," Besart said, and climbed to his feet. He reached into his pocket and removed a small business card and handed it to O'Hara. "Hotel Bacchus. Registered under the name Santino Albanese."

O'Hara nodded and slipped it into his pocket without looking at it. "I will bring her there."

Besart nodded. He turned and walked toward the main doors of the mosque. As he passed the other two men, they stood and followed him.

* * *

The hotel was tucked away on a tree-lined residential block along a hilly street in West Beirut, sandwiched between apartment buildings and facing the ocean. O'Hara entered with Valmira and told the desk attendant he was there to see Santino Albanese. The man nodded, as if expecting him, and told him to take the elevator to the top floor.

When the elevator doors opened, all three of the Albanian men that O'Hara had previously seen in the mosque, were standing in the hallway. Besart stood in the middle, and the other two were each holding pistols. The skinnier of the two men raised his gun and aimed it at O'Hara.

O'Hara flinched and reached for the Glock —

"Papa!" Valmira shouted. She lunged toward Besart.

Every instinct told him to draw the gun. But he held back.

Besart dropped to his knees and wrapped his arms around her. He caressed the back of her head and kissed her cheek, repeatedly. The girl was crying. Tears welled up in Besart's eyes, as well. He looked up at the skinny Albanian and said something in their language, at which point the man lowered the gun.

"Let's go inside," Besart said to O'Hara.

The penthouse suite took up the entire top floor of the hotel, and contained a kitchenette, multiple large couches, an expensively stocked liquor cabinet and an in-room jacuzzi. Sliding glass doors opened onto a balcony with a panoramic view of the Mediterranean Sea. A cool breeze kept the room at a comfortable temperature.

"Wine and whiskey," Besart said to the skinny man with the large nose. "Please sit," he said to O'Hara, motioning toward the couches. "What will you drink?"

"Red wine is fine," O'Hara said.

"Red," Besart said to the man, and lifted his daughter in his arms, looking at her as one might appraise a gemstone, trying to spot any imperfections. He kissed her forehead and let her down.

The powerfully built Albanian then walked over and hugged her tightly, and spoke to her in Albanian.

"This is my brother, Valdet," Besart said about the man. "Valmira was named to honor him."

O'Hara nodded. Valdet then extended his hand. O'Hara clasped it and felt the man's firm grip.

"Thank you, cousin, for rescuing her," Valdet said in English.

"My honor," O'Hara responded.

"That is Sal," Besart said, gesturing toward the skinny man. "He is my cousin. We all understand English."

Sal walked over two glasses of red wine and set them in front of O'Hara and Besart, before returning to the kitchenette, to pour more.

Besart said something to Valmira, which O'Hara understood to be about DVD movies. He looked at Valdet. "Please set her up with a film in the bedroom, so I can talk with Donovan. Come and join us, once you've got it playing." He reached out and took his daughter's hand, and spoke to her in their language.

Valmira smiled, leaned in, and kissed her father's cheek before walking toward the other room with her uncle.

Sal returned and set two more glasses of red wine on the table and then took a seat on the couch across from O'Hara. When their eyes met Sal nodded but said nothing.

"First, I want to say thank you. I owe you my life. And Sal and Valdet feel the same way." Besart raised his wine glass and held it aloft until O'Hara and Sal did the same.

They all three touched glasses and drank.

"Now, I must understand everything that you know so that I might figure out who was behind this."

Sal placed his wine down on the table and leaned forward, resting his elbows on his knees. "As you can imagine, it is very suspicious that an American in Lebanon suddenly calls and says he found Besart's daughter. Of course it is appreciated, but the story still doesn't make sense to us."

Besart sucked his teeth and waved Sal off. He then looked at O'Hara. "Tell me where and how you found her."

"I was hired by a Russian gangster to pick up a truck in northern Lebanon and drive it to his property in a town called Jounieh."

"What was this Russian's name?" Besart asked.

"Viktor Kuznetsov."

Besart glanced at Sal. "Bari?" he suggested.

Sal shrugged.

"So I drove to the location where I was supposed to pick up the truck. It was a large mansion owned by a Serbian man named Vidic."

"A Serb!" Besart said, as though it were a curse.

O'Hara nodded.

"Motherfucker," Sal hissed.

"He will be the first to die," Besart said.

"He has already been captured by Hezbollah," O'Hara said.

"When?"

"Yesterday."

"Continue," Besart said, motioning with his hand.

"So I got the truck and left the Serb's property. But something felt wrong. I didn't trust him, or the Russian. And although I still don't know why I did this, I pulled off the road, popped the door lock, and and looked inside." O'Hara suddenly realized he was not prepared to describe what he found. He swallowed the lump that had formed in his throat. "Inside the truck I found your daughter."

Besart brought his fist to his mouth and bit down on one knuckle. "What was her condition?"

"She was unconscious. From drugs. I don't know what she was given. So I called my girlfriend and asked her to come pick up Valmira and drive her to a safe location. I fastened the truck closed with a new lock and drove to the Russian's property, as he had asked me to do."

"This is Viktor Kuznetsov?" Sal asked.

O'Hara nodded. "When I got there Viktor made me open the truck in front of him. When he saw that the back was empty, I knew he would kill me."

"Then why didn't he?" Besart asked, impatiently.

"I killed him."

"What did you do with the body?" Sal asked.

"I put him in the back of the truck and closed it back up. I drove to some slums near the Beirut airport where I knew a man that helped me get rid of both the body and the truck."

"When did all of this happen?"

"Yesterday," O'Hara said. "Then I went to where my girlfriend was caring for Valmira, and we nursed her back to health."

Valdet returned and sat down on the couch in front of his untouched wine glass. He picked it up and sipped from it.

"It looks like Serbs and Russians were responsible for this," Besart told him.

Valdet looked at O'Hara as if he had been the one to say it. Then he looked at his brother. "Semenov?"

Besart glanced over but said nothing.

"Did you say Semenov?" O'Hara asked.

Valdet nodded.

"There's a guy they call the fat man who might be coming to Beirut. I think that's his last name."

"Nikolai Semenov," Besart said incredulously.

"That's him," O'Hara said.

Sal shouted something in rapid Albanian.

"I have bad blood with Nikolai Semenov over some business in Italy," Besart explained. He stood and motioned for O'Hara to do so, as well.

Besart pulled him into a tight hug and brought his mouth to O'Hara's ear. "You will tell me when you know the fat man has arrived." He squeezed O'Hara tighter, then released him. "I will go spend the rest of the night with my daughter, thanks to you." He nodded toward the table. "Drink and relax."

"I should head home," O'Hara said.

Besart nodded. Once he left the room, Valdet and Sal stood and walked O'Hara out. Nobody seemed to want to speak first as they waited in the hallway for the elevator to arrive.

"You must know something," Sal said, placing a firm grip on O'Hara's shoulder. "Besart is a very powerful man in Albania. This makes him a target for other powerful men."

"I believe it."

"Even though we are all behaving like friends and we are very grateful for what you did, if the stories you are telling us turn out to be untrue you will have worse problems than you can imagine."

"Understood," O'Hara said as the doors slid open. "You won't have to worry about that." He slapped hands with each of the men and left.

CHAPTER TWELVE

The phone vibrating against the bedside table woke O'Hara. It was a text message from Layla asking him to meet her near the Najmeh Square clock tower in downtown Beirut.

When he arrived, Layla was leaning against a light pole on the cobblestone walkway that circled the tower, dressed in a summer dress, designer sunglasses, and a floppy brimmed hat. The late morning air on that first day of August was sweltering, and O'Hara could feel the skin of his neck baking beneath the bright sun.

"What's up?" O'Hara asked, leaning in and kissing her three times on the cheeks.

"Let's sit somewhere," she said.

They walked over to a restaurant that was empty of customers and sat at an outdoor table. Layla took the seat that faced out toward the square, and O'Hara noticed her eyes darting back and forth behind her large sunglasses, scanning windows and vehicles along the street for surveillance.

They ordered glasses of mint tea and waited for the server to walk away before any words were spoken.

"What happened when you went to see Viktor, the other day?"

"I met him at Bar Sofia," O'Hara said. "He's a creep."

Layla was studying his eyes, as if to gauge his honesty.

"What did he tell you?"

"He said he would forgive me for fighting in his bar if I do some work for him."

"What type of work?"

O'Hara shrugged. "He probably wants me to hurt people. Something like that."

"He didn't say?"

O'Hara shook his head.

"Did he say when he wants you to start this work?"

O'Hara shook his head. "I haven't spoken to him since the meeting."

"Have you been spending time with Dina? She did not show up to work on Thursday."

"You know we have been hanging out."

They stopped speaking as the server returned with two glasses of tea. Once he had walked away, Layla leaned her elbows on the table and forced a smile.

"Were you the reason she did not show up to work?"

"You're all over the place with these questions. Why did you need to see me?" O'Hara asked. "I'm sure this is not about Dina."

For a long moment she sipped her tea in silence, observing him from behind her sunglasses. "Doni, you better go see Ali at the bar," she eventually said.

"When?"

"Today." She picked up a napkin and dabbed at her lips.

"Is there anything I need to know, before I go?"

"Just answer any questions he asks truthfully," she said.

"Should I head there, now?"

She nodded. "I will pay the bill."

O'Hara stood and leaned across the table to kiss her cheeks, and left. As he walked up the cobblestone path, he pulled the phone from his pocket. Keeping it low by his hip, to be less obvious should anyone be surveilling him, he sent a text message to Omar.

***

At one of the prearranged locations that they had used a few times prior, near a pedestrian alleyway that no vehicles could pass through, Omar stopped his taxi just long enough for O'Hara to climb in. He pulled the car back into traffic and followed a meandering route toward a highway that led in the direction of the airport.

"I just met with Layla," O'Hara said.

Omar kept his eyes on the road ahead and said nothing.

"She asked me if I had seen Viktor."

"She knows nothing about it," Omar said.

"Why not?" O'Hara asked.

Omar looked like he was about to answer but sighed instead and reached for a cigarette box resting in an open compartment in the center console. He used one hand to open the box and shook a cigarette free, which he snatched with his teeth. He tossed the box back, grabbed a lighter, and lit the end of his cigarette.

"I cannot get into details," he said, smoke escaping his mouth with his words. "For now, treat her as you would any other person in Lebanon. Not like your relationship with me."

"Is she no longer to be trusted?"

Omar clucked his tongue and hung his arm out the open window, flicking the ash from his cigarette. "I do not know. Something has changed." He glanced at O'Hara. "I have received nothing new from my superiors, but something is definitely different."

"You don't think she could be compromised..." O'Hara said.

Omar sighed. "Anything is possible in this line of work." He cleared his throat and spat out the window, then took a drag from his cigarette. "But despite that, I respect you. And our relationship is built upon the ability to trust one another. As you know, there are things I cannot disclose to you, but I will never betray you." He turned his head and looked at O'Hara. "I say that to you on behalf of myself, not as a member of any organization."

"Why would something have changed with her, without you knowing?"

"That is the scariest question for me to consider, *habibi*," Omar replied.

"Layla told me to go see Ali at Bar Sofia," O'Hara said.

"Then you must do that." Omar exited the highway, and entered a shantytown village of slum homes, where children were running barefoot through the intersection, kicking around a crushed soda can as if it were a soccer ball. He steered the taxi back onto a highway entrance ramp, and drove back in the direction they had come from.

Omar flicked his cigarette out the open window. "Listen, admit nothing about Viktor or the truck to anyone. I have told nobody."

"I appreciate that." He had a sick feeling in his stomach over having told the Albanians about it, and hoped their blood oaths were sincere.

"Under no circumstances."

O'Hara nodded. "Understood."

* * *

When O'Hara pulled the front door open and entered Bar Sofia, the bouncer was perched on a stool a few feet within. He stood and stepped toward O'Hara. Beyond him, Ali sat with a crowd of men in the elevated corner booth.

"You have gun?" the bouncer asked.

"None of your business," O'Hara answered.

"Give to me," the man said, and reached a hand out.

"Get your hand away from me," O'Hara said. "I'm here to see Ali."

The man stepped closer to O'Hara to block his path.

"Ali," O'Hara called out.

When he spoke, two muscular men with shaved heads walked toward him from the back corner, each with pistols drawn. When O'Hara looked over, all that remained at the elevated booth were Ali and an older, heavy-set man with a mustache, wearing a tweed walrus hat that snapped together at the brim.

"Keep your gun tucked away or you will be shot," Ali said.

"What did you want to see me about?" O'Hara asked.

"Come, sit," Ali responded.

One of the gunmen pushed O'Hara from behind, causing him to stumble. O'Hara looked back and the man shouted, "Go!"

O'Hara walked to the back corner and stood before the table.

"This is Uncle Nikolai," Ali said.

The old man said nothing. He wore a black polo shirt. A thick gold herringbone chain hung from around his neck. The whites of his eyes were bloodshot, as if someone were strangling him.

O'Hara nodded at the man. "You don't look like this guy's uncle," he said, sarcastically.

Uncle Nikolai did not answer him, nor did he smile.

"Are you being disrespectful?" Ali asked. He pulled a gun from his waist, but left his arm hanging by his side. "I will shoot you myself if you are."

O'Hara clucked his tongue, the way locals did.

"Sit," Uncle Nikolai said in accented English, nodding toward the empty seat across the table from him. He picked up a pack of Davidoff cigarettes, pulled one free, and stuck it in his mouth. He used a gold lighter to spark the end, and pulled hard. Smoke released in two streams from his nostrils.

O'Hara sat in the chair.

"Where do you come from?" the man asked.

"Boston," O'Hara said, figuring he already knew the answer.

"I have never been to the States."

"That's too bad," O'Hara said.

Uncle Nikolai tapped his cigarette on the rim of an empty tumbler glass. "More important is where I am now. Do you know why I am in Beirut?"

O'Hara shook his head.

"I am here to visit Viktor Kuznetsov. You know him, yes?"

"I assume that's the same Viktor that owns this bar."

Uncle Nikolai nodded and took a drag from his cigarette. "That one over there." He pointed a thick, stubby, ringed finger toward the bouncer. "He told us that you met with Viktor, just days ago. At this table."

"It's true," O'Hara said. "We had a few drinks."

"Would you like a drink, now?"

"Sure," O'Hara responded.

"What do you want?"

"Al Maza is fine," he said.

Uncle Nikolai looked at Ali, and gestured for him to go fetch the beer. Ali scowled at O'Hara and then walked away.

"I am going to ask you some questions," Uncle Nikolai said.

O'Hara nodded.

"I am an old man, Donovan Burke. Seventy years. If I were to travel under my real identity, there are at least two dozen countries that would arrest me and extradite me to one of three or four countries that want to put me in prison." He pointed his thick finger at O'Hara. "Yours, being one of them."

Ali returned and placed a bottle of beer and an opener on the table in front of O'Hara. O'Hara picked it up and popped the lid from the bottleneck.

"Are you not drinking anything?"

Uncle Nikolai clucked his tongue. "I never drink alcohol until all the day's business has been completed."

O'Hara picked up the beer and took a long gulp.

"So, given the circumstances that I just mentioned, I am sure you can understand why I do not like traveling anymore. There is too much risk for me, not to mention that the jet lag affects me more than it once did." He stopped speaking long enough to take a deep drag from his cigarette. He kept his deadman's gaze on O'Hara, as he blew smoke out of the side of his mouth. "And yet, despite all of that, I am here in Beirut to visit Viktor."

O'Hara swallowed more beer to avoid having to speak.

"I have not been able to reach him. Ali has not seen him in days, either."

"I haven't seen him since I sat right at this booth with him." He looked over his shoulder toward where the bouncer was sitting on his perch by the front door. "The last person in here with Viktor when I left was the meat suit, over there."

Uncle Nikolai looked over at the bouncer, then back at O'Hara.

"Are you being defensive?" Ali asked, impatiently.

O'Hara looked at Ali. "Let the adults talk."

Ali stepped toward O'Hara, who stood from his chair to face him. One of the burly Russian gunmen raised a pistol to O'Hara's cheek.

"Sit down," Uncle Nikolai said to him in a calm voice. "Ali, go sit at the bar."

Ali looked at Uncle Nikolai with a surprised expression. He walked across the room toward the bar.

"The Arabs think you have something to do with Viktor being unreachable," Uncle Nikolai said to O'Hara. "I will ask you this once more." Uncle Nikolai leaned forward as much as his large belly would allow. "Do you have any knowledge of his whereabouts?"

"I do not," O'Hara lied, maintaining eye contact with the Russian.

Uncle Nikolai pursed his lips and nodded. "That is all, then. Finish your beer and you may leave."

O'Hara turned his beer up and chugged it in large gulps until it was empty. He set it back down on the table and stood. "Thanks for the drink."

Uncle Nikolai nodded. "Will you be staying in Beirut long?"

O'Hara nodded. "Like you, I can't travel easily."

When he said this, Uncle Nikolai raised an eyebrow. "Is that so?"

O'Hara nodded.

Uncle Nikolai grinned, showing the first sign of emotion since they had met. "They will have a private booth for me, tonight. You should stop by. We can talk more about your travel situation."

"Where will this be?"

"What is the venue called?" he shouted across the bar, toward Ali.

"Catacomb," Ali called back.

"Do you know of it?" Uncle Nikolai asked O'Hara.

"No, but I will find it."

Uncle Nikolai nodded.

O'Hara shook the old Russian's plump hand and turned away. As he was walking out, he passed where Ali stood behind the bar.

"Were you with Dina on Thursday night?" Ali asked.

"Piss off," he replied.

Once on the street O'Hara let out a sigh of relief, feeling as though he had cheated death. It was his first experience in not being able to read a man's intentions. Not even in the slightest way. The entire time they spoke with one another, he didn't know if he was building rapport with Uncle Nikolai or if he was about to take an unexpected bullet in the back of the head.

He traveled along back alleys, down to the small pads of rock formation that protruded out into the ocean, below the corniche. He climbed out as far as he was able, and looked back toward the promenade. When he was sure he hadn't been followed, he pulled his phone from his pocket and dialed Besart's number.

* * *

From the street, Catacomb looked like nothing more than a derelict parking lot blocked off by metal guardrails around a giant steel floor plate, the size of a hockey rink. A modest door leading to the underground was manned by two muscular bouncers in tight shirts.

O'Hara, Dina and Amjad exited the taxi and approached the entrance. When the bouncers saw Dina, they stepped aside and opened the door. One man frisked O'Hara and Amjad to make sure they had no weapons. Nobody checked the small satchel that hung from Dina's shoulder. Amjad led the way down a dark stairwell, lit only by strips of beaded bulbs that ran along the tread of each step. At the bottom another door rattled with the hum of electronic bass music that could be heard thumping within.

The door opened to a large room of polished cement and rustic metal, with mirrored ceilings and cordoned-off crypt-like rooms recessed into the walls on two sides. The space was filled with attractive men and women, packed shoulder to shoulder and dancing to the rhythm of the DJ's melodies. On the far end of the room was a full-length bar where no less than four tenders were busy mixing drinks and serving customers.

O'Hara scanned the recessed rooms along each wall until he found one where the two men that had been at the meeting with Uncle Nikolai stood guard on either side of the doorway. He bypassed them, walked over to the bar, and ordered a round of drinks. Leaning against the bar for concealment, he removed his Glock from Dina's satchel and tucked it at the small of his back, under his shirt.

They drank with their backs to the bar, and O'Hara monitored the room with the Russian guards outside. Through the open doorway he could see a round stone table with curved booth seating. Uncle Nikolai and Ali were sitting inside with a handful of women squeezed onto the bench seating between them. Liquor and champagne bottles littered the table.

O'Hara worked up a sweat dancing with Dina, who moved her hips like she was ringing a bell, and kept him from drinking too much, too soon. Amjad drifted away from them and hovered around other men in the crowd. At some point, many songs later, he returned and draped his arms around O'Hara and Dina and shouted into their ears, "Let's drink absinthe."

At the bar, Amjad ordered a bottle of absinthe. The bartender opened a new bottle and poured three glasses. He then rested sugar cubes on flat metal spoons and laid them across the rims of the glasses. He poured water over the sugar at barely more than a drip, causing the cube to dissolve into the drink. When all three drinks were mixed, he slid the glasses across the bar.

"*Yalla!*" Amjad shouted over the music, and drained half his glass in one gulp.

O'Hara and Dina sipped theirs and winced at the burn.

"That's it for me," she said.

Amjad laughed and finished off his drink. He picked up the absinthe bottle and refilled two of the glasses. He motioned for the bartender to proceed with the sugar cubes.

O'Hara had his arm around the small of Dina's back when Ali spotted them from inside the private room. He approached the bar with a smirk on his face, and nodded at Dina.

"Where were you on Thursday?" he asked her.

O'Hara noticed Ali was grinding his teeth, and suspected he was high on something.

"Yes, sorry. I called and spoke to Layla." She looked away.

"Layla is not your boss."

"Easy, pal," O'Hara said, and pulled Dina closer to his side.

Ali looked at each of them, and grinned. "You are together, now," he said. Without waiting for an answer he focused his attention on O'Hara. "Why have you not gone to pay respect to Uncle Nikolai?"

"What am I paying respect for?" O'Hara asked.

"Arrogant American," Ali said, with a disapproving shake of his head.

"I'll go see Nikolai when I'm ready. Go mind your business."

"This isn't Boston. Do not forget that." He then turned and disappeared into the crowd.

"Asshole," O'Hara said.

Out among the dancing crowd, O'Hara spotted Valdet, standing a head taller than most others, as he made his way toward the bar. O'Hara leaned in toward Dina's ear. "I think you should head home," he said.

She pulled her head away and looked at him.

He gestured for her to lean back closer. When she did, he spoke with his lips close to her ear. "I just saw Valmira's uncle."

He looked over her shoulder, where Amjad was talking to another man who was leaning against the bar. "I would love for you to get out of here before anything crazy happens."

"Will you come?"

"You go ahead without me." He leaned in and kissed her. "Take Amjad with you."

They looked over to where Amjad was pouring a glass of absinthe for the man at the bar.

"He won't come," she said.

"Alright, I'll make him leave with me," O'Hara said. "I'll meet you at your apartment."

Dina nodded and kissed him. She turned and spoke to Amjad, who glanced at O'Hara and nodded. O'Hara and Dina walked across the dance floor toward the main entrance where they hugged once more, and she walked up the steps.

O'Hara then made his way toward the room with the two Russian guards standing on either side of the doorway. As he crossed the dance floor he felt someone bump into him.

"My bad," he said.

"Is he here?" a voice asked in English.

O'Hara turned to find Sal, Besart's cousin, standing there holding a beer.

O'Hara nodded. "I saw Valdet."

"It is just me and him. Besart's face would have been too easily recognized by Semenov." He spoke without looking at O'Hara. "He left for Albania with Valmira."

"What are you planning to do?" O'Hara asked.

"Do not worry about that. Where is he?"

"He has bodyguards."

Sal looked toward the crowd and nodded his head. O'Hara looked in the direction he had nodded, and saw Valdet standing near a group of dancing Arab women.

"I'm on my way to go see him," O'Hara said.

"Show me where he is," Sal demanded.

As O'Hara cut through the crowd, he felt an arm wrap around his neck, and for a moment he tensed up expecting a fight. A drunken giggle made him realize it was Amjad.

"Let's go have a quick drink before we get outta here," he told Amjad, and gestured toward the wall of recessed rooms.

As they approached the doorway, the two Russian guards stepped in front of them. A gruff voice shouted something in Russian, and the men parted to allow O'Hara and Amjad to pass.

"This is my friend," O'Hara said, pointing to Amjad with his thumb. "Ali knows him."

Uncle Nikolai looked at Ali, and then back at O'Hara and, nodded.

At Uncle Nikolai's insistence, they both sat along the empty end of the curved booth bench. A prostitute in a g-string with teased red hair, moved over and sat on O'Hara's lap. There were two more women sitting on either side of Uncle Nikolai, running their hands up and down his thighs. O'Hara pressed his back against the bench so she couldn't feel his gun.

"Pour them a drink," Uncle Nikolai said to Ali, who hesitated at first, and then reluctantly picked up a bottle of vodka and filled a dozen shot glasses with the liquor. Everyone in the room raised glasses.

Uncle Nikolai toasted something in Russian, and they all drank.

O'Hara gently moved the woman off his lap, and sat her beside him.

"*Habibi*," she said, in what was obviously not her native language, as she caressed his chest.

"I'm good, thanks," O'Hara replied with a smile.

"Viktor is still missing," Uncle Nikolai said to O'Hara. His bloodshot eyes had thick veins branching out from behind the lids.

"It's interesting how he had planned to present Uncle Nikolai with a special present, tonight. Yet, he is not here. Neither is his gift," Ali said.

O'Hara wanted to reach out and slap the Lebanese gangster, wondering if Viktor's present was going to be Valmira. He looked at Uncle Nikolai.

"I hope he turns up," he said. "What's back there?" He nodded toward a black door behind where the Russian sat.

"Stairs to the street," Uncle Nikolai said.

"Do you think we come in and out of clubs like the rest of you?" Ali said, and laughed.

When nobody laughed with him, he turned and grabbed the breast of the nearest prostitute. She giggled and he winked at her.

"Would you like to work for Ali?" Uncle Nikolai asked. "Until I figure out what is going on with Viktor, he will be taking on more responsibility."

"I appreciate the offer," O'Hara replied. "But I won't work for this man."

"Watch your tongue," Ali said. He removed a black pistol from his waist and rested it on the table.

"Put that away," Uncle Nikolai said.

Ali tucked it back in his pants.

Sudden arguing could be heard outside the doorway. O'Hara turned his head in time to see Valdet cold cock one of the Russian guards with a heavy fist, dropping the man against the base of the cement wall. The second guard tackled Valdet to the ground, drawing a gun and pressing it to the back of his head.

As the brawl escalated outside the doorway, Ali and the prostitutes all rose from their seats in a state of confusion, as did O'Hara and Amjad. Uncle Nikolai stayed put. O'Hara noticed Sal appear through the doorway, maneuvering his narrow frame among the prostitutes. When he reached the table, he slid on one knee across the curved booth bench to where Uncle Nikolai sat. He brought his hand to his mouth and spat into it. In one fluid motion he dragged a small razor blade across the old Russian's thick neck.

Bright red blood sprayed across the wall like a stripe of graffiti. Ali drew his gun as the prostitutes fled the room. Before he could aim his shot, Sal swung his arm in a backhanded motion and ran the blade across Ali's face. He flailed his arm and the gun went off in his hand.

O'Hara had been reaching for his own gun when Ali's shot fired. The sound was deafening. He drew his Glock and aimed it at Ali, just as Sal swiped his blade again and cut the Lebanese gangster's throat. Another gunshot went off outside the room. One of the Russian guards rushed in with his gun aimed at Sal. O'Hara raised the Glock and shot the man in the head, dropping him beside Ali's lifeless body.

O'Hara looked over at Uncle Nikolai, who was reclined in the booth, still reaching one hand for the open gash along the side of his neck. His shirt was drenched in blood, and his dull eyes stared up at the ceiling. A groan came from the floor. O'Hara looked down. It was Amjad, holding his arm, bleeding.

"You're hit?"

"My arm," he said, and released a painful wail.

Outside the doorway, the crowd stampeded toward the main exits. O'Hara knelt down and helped Amjad to his feet, and watched Sal slip out of the room. A bloodcurdling scream followed. Sal reappeared and shouted at O'Hara, "Valdet is dead!"

O'Hara grabbed Amjad by his good arm and dragged him past Uncle Nikolai's body, toward the black door.

"Where are you going?" Sal hollered.

"This door leads to the street," O'Hara answered. He opened the door and the three of them climbed a dark, narrow stairwell to a second door. They emerged at the far end of the parking lot as police and emergency vehicles screeched to a stop in front of the main entrance to the club. A large crowd swarmed the street as people continued to spill through the doorway, crying and calling for missing friends.

O'Hara took off his outer shirt and draped it over Amjad's shoulders to conceal his bleeding arm.

Amjad was wincing, with his wounded arm hanging limp, and his other hand keeping pressure on the bullet hole.

"Were you hit anywhere else?" O'Hara asked.

"I don't think so," Amjad answered.

O'Hara felt a hand grip his arm. He turned to find Sal standing behind him.

"If you are ever in Albania, go to Himare and find Besart," he said.

Before O'Hara could say anything, the thin man turned and crossed the tree-lined street, where he vanished among the shadows.

CHAPTER THIRTEEN

"Beirut has survived many wars and has partied through every one of them," Omar said, and took a drag from his cigarette. "It is how the Lebanese people tolerate a life that always threatens to end at any moment. This shooting will not bring the city to a halt, the way it would in the States."

They were parked a few blocks from O'Hara's flat, kitty-cornered to a white stone mosque. The azan had just sounded, and the two of them watched through the taxi windows as observant Muslims began to enter the building.

"The show will go on," Omar added, and then looked at O'Hara. "How many were killed? Five, six?"

"Something like that," O'Hara responded.

"All Russians, right? And one Albanian?"

"And Ali," O'Hara said.

Omar cleared his throat and spit out the window. He pulled from his cigarette.

"He was a pretender," he said with disdain. "What's the American phrase, a want to be?"

"Wannabe," O'Hara said.

"Yes. Ali was a wannabe Ali Hassan Salameh."

"I don't know who that is."

"He was a real gangster. A worthy adversary." Omar flicked his cigarette butt out the window. "We took him out here, in Beirut."

"We?"

Omar nodded. "Listen, when you go to the party today, I need you to pay very close attention to Layla, if she is there."

"What am I supposed to be watching for?"

"Anything out of the ordinary. Pay attention to the people she makes time to speak with. Things like that."

"Have you learned anything more about what we talked about, regarding her?"

Omar clucked his tongue.

"I'll let you know if I notice anything," O'Hara said.

Omar nodded. "Go wash the blood off you, and get some sleep."

O'Hara opened the taxi door, and climbed out.

***

The interior cabin of the yacht was air conditioned and smelled of strong coffee and burning incense. O'Hara had barely slept since leaving Omar that morning, and the dimness of the lighting should have made him drowsy, but he was wired with nervous energy.

Amjad was high on pain-killers and had taken the trouble to dress in a traditional robe, like the few other Saudi men in the room. His wounded arm was secured across his chest by a sling. The skin of his face was pale, and he was unshaven.

They were sitting beside one another in oversized chairs, even more luxurious than the last time they had been invited to the upper cabin. Across from them sat Prince Ahmed and a fourth chair, which was empty. Ship crew members stood in silence in the background, as waiters presented trays of tea and pastries.

Prince Ahmed spoke in Arabic to Amjad who nodded his head in reply. The Prince then looked at O'Hara and smiled. "Forgive me for not speaking English in front of you."

"Prince, this is your yacht," O'Hara said. He accepted a glass mug of tea from one of the waiters. Another waiter held out an ornate silver tray, from which he picked a piece of baklava with a fine cloth napkin.

The loud rumbling of a helicopter could be heard, and the walls and floor began to vibrate. Neither the prince or the guards seemed concerned. The rumbling grew louder, until the chandeliers that hung from the ceiling started rattling. Prince Ahmed and Amjad stood from their chairs. O'Hara did the same.

The noise stopped as the door at the far end of the room opened and four Arab soldiers entered. Two of them carried assault rifles slung over their shoulders. They scanned the room and stepped away from one another to make way for a fifth man. When O'Hara saw who it was, he was taken aback.

The large, bearded man dressed in a pressed white robe and starched ghutra headscarf needed no introduction. O'Hara had seen the man's face many times, in magazines and on television screens. The man walked toward them with a relaxed gait and a casual smile on his face. When he reached them, he kissed Prince Ahmed on both cheeks, and then did the same to Amjad, saying something to him in Arabic, and gently touching his shoulder. He turned to O'Hara and extended his hand.

"It's an honor, your Highness," O'Hara said, addressing the man by the honorific he had been told to use. They clasped each other's hands.

The Crown Prince replied with a nod, and gestured with an open hand for him to sit.

Waiters returned with trays of tea and pastries which the Crown Prince accepted. He sipped from his tea and looked at O'Hara.

"Allow me to apologize in advance," the Crown Prince said in a gruff voice, in accented English. "But I will not stay long. There is important business I must tend to before heading back to the Kingdom." He held up an open palm. "While I was in the area, I wanted to meet to thank you in person for protecting Amjad. Prince Ahmed has spoken highly of you."

"Thank you for taking the time to be here," O'Hara said.

"It seems that most of the victims of the attack were Russians. Did you know these men?"

"Some of them I'd met before."

"And they are the reason you were both in the private room when the shooting occurred," the Crown Prince confirmed.

O'Hara nodded.

"One of the dead men is Nikolai Semenov. I know of this man."

O'Hara nodded, again.

"Do we know who killed him?"

O'Hara shook his head. "Sorry."

"There was an Albanian man among the dead," the Crown Prince said.

"I heard that, also," O'Hara said.

"I suppose the question is whether the Albanian was with the Russians, or was one of the attackers." The Crown Prince sipped his tea, then flashed a goofy grin. "I watch too many American homicide shows. What is most important is that Amjad is alive, thanks to you."

O'Hara said nothing.

"He is a wild child, as you Americans say, and his behavior has caused us more than a few headaches." The Crown Prince shot a sideways glance at Amjad, "But he is Prince Ahmed's blood. And because of what you have done for him, please consider us at your service." He placed a large hand on Prince Ahmed's knee. "Prince Ahmed will give you his contact information and if you ever need anything, simply ask."

O'Hara touched his hand to his chest. "That means more to me than you know."

"Amjad will return to the Kingdom with me so that he may be cared for by our doctors while he heals." The Crown Prince pointed at him. "If you ever want to come visit, we would be pleased to host you."

O'Hara nodded, patting his chest once more.

The Crown Prince grabbed a napkin off one of the waiter's trays and wiped his hands before standing from his chair. When he did this the other three men stood, as well. He extended his arm before O'Hara, who clasped his hand. "I hope to see you again, *insha'allah*."

O'Hara replied with a slight bow of his head.

"*Yalla*," the Crown Prince said to Amjad and draped a thick arm over his shoulder, continuing to speak in the rapid, guttural sounds of his native dialect.

As the two men walked toward the exit, Amjad reached his hand out and grabbed O'Hara's. He gave a squeeze of thanks, then let go. When he said nothing, O'Hara winked.

"I will travel with them," Prince Ahmed said to O'Hara and kissed him on both cheeks. He handed over a small business card, with a series of both Arabic and English numerals. "This is my personal phone number." He walked away, following behind the Crown Prince and Amjad.

O'Hara slipped the card into his pocket.

* * *

O'Hara returned to the lounge chair beside Dina. He was drinking a Bedouin-style tea from the bar. The pool was crowded with guests and the music was playing as if it were any other Sunday. Omar was right, O'Hara thought. Maybe life in Beirut just carried on, after all.

"Where's Amjad?" Dina asked.

"He left," O'Hara said.

"On the helicopter?"

O'Hara nodded and tested his tea. "You'll never guess whose ride that was."

"The Crown Prince?"

O'Hara looked at her and laughed.

"What did you think of him?"

"I won't be accepting any invitations to the consulate in Istanbul, but he was pleasant."

Dina stared at him over the rims of her sunglasses.

"What's wrong?" O'Hara asked.

"I hope Amjad wasn't headed to the consulate in Istanbul, as you say."

O'Hara looked up at the sky. "He'll be fine." He turned and studied her. "What's on your mind?"

"I am done with Lebanon," she said, then closed her eyes and leaned back to feel the warmth of the sun on her face.

"You and me both," he said.

"Will you leave with me?" she asked.

"Yes," he said. "I plan on being wherever you are, from here on out."

She turned her head toward him and smiled, but did not speak.

The electronic music grew louder and some of the guests were dancing on the upper deck. All the lounge chairs now had bodies on them, and more people were arriving at the back stairwell.

O'Hara noticed Layla enter onto the deck. She was wearing oversized sunglasses, a loosely draped cotton dress, and wedges. Behind her stood the American man, Billy Richter. Layla spotted O'Hara and Dina and walked in their direction, while Richter took a different path, stopping to greet a few people on his way toward the bar.

Layla leaned down and kissed each of their cheeks. She then sighed and shook her head, as she looked around for an empty lounge chair. There were none, so O'Hara stood from his and insisted she sit.

"Thank you," she said as she sat. "Last night..." she added, leaving the sentence unfinished.

O'Hara nodded.

"I was just arriving when everyone came rushing out." She ran her hand through her hair. "Was it bad?"

"It wasn't good," he said. "I'm guessing you heard about Ali."

Layla nodded her head. "And Viktor still hasn't shown his face," she said. "It makes me wonder if he has anything to do with it."

O'Hara was unable to gauge her sincerity.

Layla lay back in the chair. "I need a drink."

"I'll make a run," O'Hara said.

"You're a darling," she said. "I'll take a rum and coke."

O'Hara nodded. He looked at Dina.

"No thanks," she said.

"Be back in a few," O'Hara said, and leaned down and kissed Dina on the cheek. With his mouth near her ear, he whispered, "Don't trust her." Then he walked away.

At the bar O'Hara was waiting for Layla's drink when someone leaned over his shoulder and said, "We gotta talk, buddy." He turned to find Billy Richter standing beside him, looking at the bartender, as though he had not been the one who spoke.

"About what?" O'Hara asked.

"Is the drink for you, or your lady friend?"

"The lady friend you showed up with."

"Have a waiter run it over to her and meet me on the upper deck." Richter got the bartender's attention and held up a fresh cigar, then spoke to the man in flawless Arabic. He turned to O'Hara. "It's important."

The bartender handed Richter a lighter, and the American walked away. When the bartender slid Layla's drink across the counter to O'Hara, he picked it up and grabbed the wrist of a waiter who was walking past. He pointed out where Layla and Dina sat, and asked him to bring the drink over. He fished a bill out of his pocket as a tip. Then he walked upstairs.

Richter was leaning against a railing near the raised DJ booth, beside a large subwoofer that was as tall as he was. He was puffing on the cigar, and when O'Hara approached him, he offered him an unlit one. O'Hara took the cigar and bit the end off with his teeth and spat it off the edge of the boat, before sticking it in his mouth and accepting the lighter. He lit the end and took a few puffs.

"Do we have to be next to this thing?" he asked, gesturing toward the subwoofer.

"In case the Saudis have any bugs planted," Richter said. "What you and I have to talk about can't be heard."

O'Hara said nothing.

Richter slipped his hand in his pocket and pulled out a photograph, offering it to O'Hara. It was a headshot of a thick-necked man with short brown hair and a beard.

"Know who that is?" Richter asked.

"Nope," O'Hara answered.

"That's Donovan Burke of Dorchester, Boston."

O'Hara glanced up at him.

"He's dead, of course. But that was him."

"What are you getting at?"

"I think you know," Richter said.

"Who do you really work for?" O'Hara asked.

"I think you have an idea of that, too," Richter said.

"So what do you want?"

Richter slipped his hand into his other pocket, and removed a smart phone. He tapped the screen several times with his index finger, and then offered it to O'Hara. "Read that. Tell me if you recognize anyone."

O'Hara looked at the phone screen, where an article was written in Hebrew.

"I can't read this shit," he said, and handed the phone back.

"Hang on," Richter said. He tapped his finger a few more times, and handed the phone to O'Hara. "There."

O'Hara began to read an English language article from an Israeli news website that talked about how an American right-wing terrorist cell was taken into custody by the Shin-Bet, in an Israeli settlement near the Golan Heights. As he read, and scrolled down on the screen, he eventually came to recognize the mugshot photographs of some of the men he had known in Idaho. His heart skipped a beat.

O'Hara looked up from the phone at Richter, who nodded, and pulled from his cigar causing the muscles of his sinewy neck to flex as he did so.

"This morning. I don't think it's hit American outlets yet, but in case you haven't heard, Preston Knox is in custody, as well. Back stateside."

"I dunno what you're talking about. What's this have to do with me?"

"Don't bullshit," Richter said. "I know why you're out here." He took the phone back from O'Hara, and held it up between them. "And I know who sent you here."

O'Hara had been interrogated by too many New York cops, and knew better than to make the mistake of confirming or denying anything. His mind raced to connect the dots, realizing that if Shin-Bet had detained the men in the news article, it meant that Yoni Kaplan didn't protect them. Or couldn't.

"What are you, a spook?" he asked.

"As the Lord said to Moses, I am what I am," Richter replied. "And you are what you are, O'Hara Poit."

O'Hara looked away and took a drag from his cigar.

"You were sent out here to meet your old friend Jared Ingleton." Richter smiled. "You will stand down on that mission. What Ingleton is involved in is way above your head."

O'Hara kept a stone face. He wondered if the American was implying that the United States government was behind the Russian trained, black nationalist militia, or if maybe Richter, himself, was Red's direct handler.

"What three-letter crew are you with?" he asked.

"Don't talk like that out here," Richter responded. "Just know that your hands are tied. You either walk away from Ingleton, or I can have you sent home, where you are now wanted for violating your parole." He chewed on the end of his cigar without smoking it. "You're a fugitive, my friend."

O'Hara flashed an easy smile. Like none of this bothered him. "And if I walk away, what happens?"

Richter shook his head. "You just keep living your life with your pretty little lady down there." He gestured toward the pool deck, below. "As long as you lay low, I could give a shit what happens to you here in Lebanon."

O'Hara's phone vibrated in his pocket. "Hang on," he said and pulled the phone out and looked at it, not recognizing the number on the screen. He tapped the answer button and held the phone to his ear.

"Hello," he said.

"Yo," Red's voice responded.

"What's up?" he asked, smiling at Richter while he spoke.

"We gotta meet. I can probably free up about twenty minutes tomorrow."

"Okay," O'Hara said.

"We are getting ready to move out," Red said.

"Oh?"

"Can you meet up here in the Bekaa, tomorrow?"

"Yep," he said.

"You can't talk right now, can you?" Red asked.

"Nope."

"Okay, I'll call you in the morning."

"Cool," O'Hara responded.

"Bet."

O'Hara hung up the phone, and slipped it back into his pocket.

"Who was that?"

"Your mother," O'Hara replied.

Richter grinned.

"Are we done, here?"

Richter nodded. "Just remember, buddy. I'm watching you now."

"Sure, pal," O'Hara said, and stubbed his cigar out against the railing. He then handed it to Richter and walked away.

Down on the pool deck, O'Hara sat on the lounge chair at Dina's feet. "I think I'm gonna get out of here. Last night is beginning to catch up to me."

"I'll come with you," Dina said. She stood and picked up her shirt.

"You hear about the arrest?" O'Hara asked Layla.

"What arrest?" she asked.

He stared at her, but did not respond. He stood, and leaned close to Dina's ear.

"Do you remember that American guy we met in the pool last week, who works in the embassy?"

She nodded her head.

"He's walking across the deck, on the other side of the pool. I need you to snap a photo of him on your phone."

She found Richter with her eyes while pulling her shirt over her head.

O'Hara leaned down and kissed Layla on the cheeks, and said, "I'll catch up with you later."

Dina said goodbye to Layla, and walked ahead of O'Hara toward the stairs that led down to the rear of the yacht. Billy Richter was busy talking to an Arab man by the lounge chairs a few yards from where she walked. When O'Hara turned to follow, he saw that she had her phone in her hand.

CHAPTER FOURTEEN

They were lying together in bed. Wooden exterior shutters were pulled closed over the windows and all the lights were off in the home to give it the appearance of being unoccupied. The low-hanging sun cast sheets of orange light through the wooden battens. It enabled O'Hara to make out the curves of Dina's body where she lay with her back to him.

"What will you do with this property when we leave?"

"Lock it up and let my parents know I've gone." Dina rolled over to face him and used her finger to trace the scar across his chest. "They can decide what happens with it."

"It might take me a while to get to a place like Australia, with all my hang-ups. I need to figure a way out of Lebanon, first."

"You will," she said.

He reached out and took hold of her hand and lifted it to his lips. "My psychic," he said and kissed it. He then sat up, abruptly.

"What's wrong?"

"You just gave me an idea."

She raised one eyebrow, waiting.

"Would you feel comfortable meeting Red instead of me?"

She shrugged. "I guess I can. But why?"

"After hearing everything that guy Richter seems to know about this whole situation, something just feels too risky for Red and me to chance being spotted together. I don't trust Richter at all. We can throw a disguise on you much easier than on me, and to be honest I've come to trust your gut as much as my own, anyway."

"I can meet him if it is what you want," she said.

He set his coffee on the bedside table, then took hold of her cup and did the same with it. He moved closer and lay beside her in silence. There was no point in trying to put her mind at ease with reassurances or promises he might not keep. Her intuition was on a level he had never encountered before, and she likely had a better awareness of what was to come than he could offer. Realizing that, however, did not prevent him from bearing heavy guilt for dragging her into the convoluted web that had become his world. It did not relieve him of the obligation to shield her from any danger that came with it. He listened to her slow breathing until he was sure she had fallen asleep, wishing he could just run away from it all to begin a new life with her, far away from everyone involved.

* * *

He was still awake the next morning when his phone vibrated on the bedside table.

He answered it. "Hey."

"There is a *souq* in Baalbek. A bazaar-type neighborhood. How soon can you get there?"

"I'm about forty minutes from the town," O'Hara replied. "What's up?"

"That works."

"You all good?" O'Hara asked.

"Yeah. I gotta get off this phone, though. Can you be there in forty?"

"Yeah."

"There's a corner shop in one of the pedestrian pathways with a sign that reads *Kerman* in English letters. It sells all kinds of tin coffeepots and tea kettles, and shit. You can ask anyone where it is and they'll know. Go find that joint and browse inside like you're shopping."

"Alright, but hey, I got rolled up on yesterday. I don't think me and you should risk being spotted together."

"Then why are we wasting our time, talking? I need to get off this phone."

"I'm going to send a woman to meet you. You can trust her, one hundred. Wifey."

"Wifey?" Red asked.

"Yeah."

"Bro, I'm trusting you with my life. Promise me this isn't a trap."

"On Nan, it's not."

"Okay."

"You'll meet her, then?"

"Yeah," Red said. "Send wifey to Kerman. I'll be there."

* * *

O'Hara parked the Nissan along a dusty lane that led to the bazaar, which Dina knew well from family shopping trips as a child. She was dressed as an observant Muslim in a black abaya gown with a *niqab* veil covering her face. They had bought it at a roadside shop just outside of Zahle as an extra layer of security, in case of surveillance.

He watched her walk up the lane and disappear around the corner into the busy souk. He was wearing a lightweight traditional scarf around his neck, and a pair of large aviator sunglasses. He reclined in the driver's seat and pretended to sleep. Should any locals take an interest he hoped to look like an innocent man pulled over for a quick nap.

In reality, behind the shades, his eyes were wide open and taking note of the face of every person he saw up ahead in the bazaar intersection. After about twenty minutes, he noticed Dina come back into view from around the corner. She walked toward the vehicle, holding a small, copper Turkish coffee pot. She climbed in and pulled the door shut. O'Hara turned the Nissan around in the alley, and retraced the route he had taken into the town.

"How'd it go?" he asked once they were back on the main boulevard, driving beneath the rows of yellow and green Hezbollah flags toward Zahle.

"He seems to care a great deal about you," Dina said. Her eyes were misty, as if she were holding back emotions. "Too much."

"What did he say?"

"He said his group will be leaving Lebanon tomorrow, along with some Hezbollah commandos. They are boarding a ship at the port of Beirut and will make their way to Cyprus, where they will fly to Canada. From there he believes they will be smuggled across the border into the United States. He thinks Montana."

"The Hezbollah guys, too?" O'Hara wondered if it was coincidence that he had initially flown to Cyprus in order to be smuggled into Lebanon by boat.

Dina nodded. "He said you need to tell whoever you are working with about this. He will not have any contact with his American handler until he is back in the States, and by then he is afraid it will be too late to stop whatever plan is put into motion." She looked at her lap. "It is something big. Those were his exact words."

O'Hara stared at the road ahead. He took note of the cars in his rearview mirrors, not seeing any that seemed to be following him.

"Did you show him the photo on your phone?" he asked.

"Yes. He said he knew the man. He said he goes by the name Jack, and he occasionally visits their training base where he meets with the Russians in charge." Dina looked over. "He said he gets the impression that he's some kind of financial backer."

O'Hara looked over at her. "Jack?"

Dina nodded. "He told us Billy, right?"

"Billy Richter," O'Hara said. "Once Red takes off on that boat, we need to get out of this country while we still can. While I still can."

"He said one more thing to me before I left him," Dina said.

"What's that?"

"He said to tell you that he would never betray you. And never will."

O'Hara felt an unexpected wave of emotion crash over him, and he took a deep breath to keep from choking up.

"That he will see you back home."

O'Hara nodded. He knew that was unlikely and it left him feeling empty.

"He asked to see my face so that he could know what I look like, because he could hear in your voice over the phone that you love me."

When he glanced over at her, she was looking at him. He reached his hand out and held hers. "I do," he said. "Very much."

* * *

When they returned to the house in Zahle, they locked the doors and windows and laid low for the rest of the day into the evening.

They opened the last bottle of red wine from the cabinet, hoping to calm their nerves, and discussed possible ways O'Hara might bypass authorities and escape Lebanon without leaving a trail. By the time they had finished the wine, they had yet to come up with a viable plan. His phone rang. He answered.

"Poet," a man's voice said in heavily accented English.

"Who's this?"

"An old friend," the voice responded. "Let's not name names over an insecure phone line."

O'Hara knew who it was. There were only a handful of people who ever called him by that name, and only one he could think of with an accent.

"I want you to meet me tomorrow in Beirut," Yoni Kaplan said.

"I thought you don't come across the border," O'Hara replied.

"Tomorrow, I will." Yoni paused. "Hire a taxi outside your flat at seventeen-thirty. He will know where to take you."

"What's that, five-thirty?"

"Precisely."

"I'm guessing this is important," O'Hara said, with the intonation of a question.

"See you tomorrow," Yoni replied, and disconnected the line.

O'Hara laid the phone down on the lounge-room coffee table, and looked at Dina.

"I have to go down to Beirut to meet someone, tomorrow. I'd like it if you stayed here."

She nodded. "There's a bad energy surrounding all of this. I do not like the idea of you going back there at the moment."

O'Hara sighed. "This could be my way out of the country, though. Let's sleep on it."

They walked up to the master bedroom, undressed, and climbed beneath the sheets. She tried to comfort him using her body, but O'Hara could not bring himself to make love to her. His mind was overcome by anxiety and worry, attempting to connect all the moving parts of what was going on. He stared at the pinstripe patches of moonlight that hovered beyond the drawn window shutters. It could not be a coincidence that Yoni would come to Beirut on the same day that Red's crew was shipping out.

CHAPTER FIFTEEN

The air was crisp as they rode down out of the mountains. Dina drove. O'Hara closed his eyes and leaned his head through the open window, feeling the wind against his face and breathing it in deeply. He felt the tickle of nervousness in his stomach, unsure of what the meeting with Yoni might entail. Of the two other Israelis he knew in the country, one of them no longer trusted the other. That the one he still trusted was the one who would chauffeur him to the meeting was a positive sign. But he had no way discerning truth from deception anymore.

He reminded himself that by nightfall Red would have left Lebanon, and once that had occurred there would be no more reason to stay. With any luck he could then shed the skin of Donovan Burke.

Dina dropped him off two blocks away from his flat. He kissed her and made her promise to drive straight back to Zahle. He stopped by the bakery to see Anwar and Mona, and bought a coffee, two boiled eggs and a tray of baklava, and took it all upstairs.

When he entered the flat, the small tells he had set up in the door to know whether someone had been inside, were missing. He had expected as much, and for that reason left nothing important inside. He could think of at least four different groups of people that would have enough interest to break into his home. And each of them were dangerous.

Knowing he needed to calm his nerves, he did pushups and shadowboxed for the next hour. He showered and climbed into bed, where he passed time by trying to visualize what a future with Dina might look like outside of Lebanon. He was too wired to sleep.

At four-thirty, he got up and scanned the windows of the buildings and storefronts across the narrow street, and watched the pedestrian traffic below. He noticed nothing out of the ordinary.

By five-thirty he stepped out of the small door beside the bakery onto the sidewalk. He raised his arm for a taxi as he stepped off the curb, and Omar's Peugeot pulled alongside him and stopped. He climbed in and they drove off.

"What's this about?" O'Hara asked him. "To draw Yoni to this side of the border?"

"The militia is on the move," Omar said.

O'Hara looked out the window at the now-familiar scenery as Omar took them on a meandering route toward East Beirut. "We will drive a bit longer this time," Omar said, while glancing at each of his rearview mirrors. "We have to be especially careful about surveillance today."

"Yeah," O'Hara replied.

"Layla is down there," Omar said. "I am headed there, too, once I drop you off."

"To the port?"

Omar nodded.

"Are you busting them?"

"*Shoo*?" he asked, and glanced at O'Hara.

"Are you detaining them?"

Omar clucked his tongue. "I am only there to watch Layla's back from a distance. She will be there with the American you asked about."

"I don't like that guy," O'Hara said.

"Layla has a relationship with him that I cannot make sense of."

O'Hara was not sure that Omar knew as little as he pretended.

"I can't wait to get out of this country," he said.

Omar nodded.

"Do you think Yoni will help me leave?"

"It's worth asking him," Omar said.

He steered the taxi around a corner and doubled back in the direction they had come. He then turned south, taking a detour through a series of slums before returning to the corniche, passing the battle-scarred Holiday Inn, and up the hill into the same neighborhood that O'Hara's flat was in. He pulled up in front of a high-rise building with an awning and sliding glass doors that opened to a marble lobby, where an oversized chandelier hung from the ceiling.

"Take the elevator to the twelfth floor," Omar said. "Apartment four."

O'Hara extended his arm. "Thanks," he said.

Omar kissed his own palm and clasped O'Hara's hand.

* * *

He found number four and knocked on the door. A moment later it swung inward, and Yoni Kaplan stood there wearing glasses with a bristly gray beard covering his face. He clasped O'Hara's hand and welcomed him inside.

The apartment was clear of furniture aside from a few chairs set around a circular table. A pale blue bottle of Bombay Sapphire gin rested on the table beside a bottle of tonic water, a dish of lemon slices, and two empty glasses. A sliding balcony door was left open in the main room through which a warm breeze blew in from the sea. The balcony offered a panoramic view of the city to the east.

"I've been eager to know what could be important enough to bring you here," O'Hara said.

Yoni smiled and took the two glasses to the kitchen where he opened the freezer door and scooped ice cubes into them.

"I am like an old ghost who returns to haunt this city, from time to time," Yoni said. He carried the glasses to the table and filled them with gin and tonic water, then dropped a lemon slice into each. He handed one to O'Hara and glanced at his wristwatch. "How has your time in Lebanon been?"

"It's been real," O'Hara replied and took a sip of his drink.

Yoni looked beyond O'Hara's shoulder toward the balcony. "Look at that," he said.

O'Hara turned around, to see a large black plume of smoke rising from a point along the coast in the distance.

"Looks like a fire," Yoni said.

"That'd be my guess," O'Hara said. "Black smoke." When he studied the plume more closely, he could see little flashes of white among the billowing dark column. "What do you think those little flashes are?"

When he turned to Yoni for the answer, the Israeli was staring at his watch again. "Don't know," he said, and walked toward the balcony. "Let's have a closer look."

O'Hara followed him out.

"So you made contact with Ingleton?" Yoni said.

"I did."

O'Hara noticed flames at the base of the smoke plume licking up toward the sky. Sirens blared in the distance.

"And?" Yoni asked.

"It's pretty much as I'm sure your people reported back to you. He's a top dog in the crew that's being trained by the Volk Group."

"Are you aware that they're leaving Lebanon, today?" Yoni asked.

O'Hara observed the way the Israeli watched the fire in the distance.

"No," he lied. "Where are they headed?"

"Canada," Yoni said. "If I were to guess, I would say that fire is occurring at the port they're planning to leave from."

O'Hara looked at the expanding cloud of smoke, then back at Yoni.

"That's no coincidence, is it?"

Yoni's lips curled into a grin. "You Americans only think in conspiracy theories, don't you? Just like Preston Knox. Everything must have some hidden truth beyond what is obvious to the five senses."

"Speaking of Preston," O'Hara said. "What's the deal with his arrest? And your country detaining the others? You let that happen?"

"They went rogue, my friend." Yoni glanced at his watch, then sipped his drink. "They were freelancing, planning to enter Lebanon. It risked ruining the entire operation if they were caught, killed, or drew attention to a western presence in any way."

"So you arrested them and drew even more attention?"

Yoni nodded. "But if you read any of the Israeli news stories, they were American white supremacists. Fueled by fundamentalist Christian, alt-right motivations. There is no mention of African-American militias."

"Preston won't keep his mouth shut."

"Right about now Preston has his hands full trying to justify the arsenal he was sitting on out in Idaho, and why his community was harboring at least a dozen convicted criminal fugitives. Do you think you're the only ex-convict he sent out on a mission?" Yoni clucked his tongue. "You should have seen what he had going on in Mexico before you met him. Trust me, with everything falling on Preston's head right now, he will be no threat to what we are trying to accomplish out here."

"Why are you still interested in the militia if they are going to Canada? They won't be a threat to your country from there."

"They are traveling with a battle-hardened unit of Hezbollah commandos. They will be smuggled into your country along with Ingleton's unit, where they'll target Israeli embassies within the states." He removed his eyeglasses and slipped on sunglasses from his breast pocket. Pointing to the pair that rested atop O'Hara's head, he said, "The sun in the Middle East is very damaging to one's eyes. Those are doing no good resting up on your forehead."

O'Hara lowered his sunglasses. "The sun and everything else in this crazy country." He'd been waiting for Yoni to mention something about Viktor or Nikolai Semenov, but the Israeli did not. "So why haven't I been detained with the rest of the Idaho crew?"

Yoni let out a short laugh. "You were ensnared by them, but you are not one of them. I watched what you've done while here in Beirut. Most of which you haven't mentioned to me." He glanced at his wristwatch, and then at the sky above. "I believe you can be very useful to me if you stay here." He knelt down on one knee and grabbed hold of the iron railing that ran along the top of the cement terrace wall. "Grip that railing and kneel."

He was watching the smoke in the distance. The plume had doubled in width.

O'Hara looked toward the fire as the entire horizon lit up in a blinding flash of white, followed by a wave of hot air pressure, that knocked both men onto their backs. O'Hara heard a loud thunderous noise but was unsure of whether it came before or after impact. He rolled to his side, disoriented, feeling at his back to make sure the Glock was still in place. He looked over at Yoni, who had climbed to his hands and knees. His sunglasses had been blown from his head. O'Hara felt for his. They were gone, too.

"Are you alright?" O'Hara asked, shaking his head to clear the feeling of cobwebs within.

Yoni nodded. He got his feet under him and stumbled back into the apartment. When O'Hara stood, he noticed the glass panes of the sliding doors and windows were all cracked or shattered. Over his shoulder, he stared out into a cloud of swirling gray where the skyline of the city had once been. There was a humming sound in his head. He entered the apartment.

"What the fuck just happened?" O'Hara rasped, as Yoni rubbed his ears.

"One thing that is certain..." he gasped. "The man who sent you to prison was down there." He picked up the bottle of gin and sipped from it, then hissed. "And some Hezbollah terrorists."

O'Hara imagined Red down at the seat of the explosion. His breath caught in his throat.

"And countless other innocent people," O'Hara said. "Layla?"

Yoni glanced at him. "Don't pretend to know Layla."

"Omar," O'Hara said.

Yoni coughed and staggered slightly, then regained balance. "This is all bigger than your mind can absorb." He held up a finger in the air. "Nothing is what you have been led to believe. Nothing."

O'Hara felt stunned. He thought of Dina and the last thing Red had said to her. How he never had, and never would betray him.

"Come, we will cross the border and regroup while the dust settles over here."

Yoni turned toward the door leading out of the apartment. O'Hara tapped the small of his back and located his gun. He could not hear himself think over the persistent humming sound in his head. He drew the Glock, aimed it behind Yoni's ear, and pulled the trigger.

***

Downstairs, on the street, there were people crying and hugging one another, staring up at the smoke-stained sky. O'Hara turned from the front entrance of the building and made his way up the hill. He wanted to get as far away from there as possible before he called Dina. A white car pulled up beside him and screeched to a halt, jumping the curb with one of its front tires. The driver's side door opened and Omar climbed out, his face covered in soot.

O'Hara drew his gun and aimed it. Omar paused, then drew his own pistol in one fluid movement.

"What the fuck have you people done?" O'Hara hissed.

"Us people?! Where is that bastard?!" Omar demanded.

"I was knocked out by the blast." O'Hara gestured over his shoulder. "Yoni was gone when I came to."

Omar lowered his gun and walked toward the building, leaving the car's engine running and the front door open.

"Where are you going?"

"Yoni sent me down there knowing what would happen. I will kill him." Omar turned to limp down the hill toward the apartment building.

"There's no one there," O'Hara called out.

Omar stopped and looked back. He limped back to O'Hara, who held his gun down by his side. He knew he couldn't take aim quicker than Omar could, so he didn't bother to try.

"But you're right. He knew the blast was going to happen," he said, with a nod.

Omar studied his eyes for a long moment. "Get in the car. *Yalla!*"

They drove out of Beirut, neither of them saying a word. O'Hara noticed exposed wires below the steering wheel and knew the vehicle had been stolen.

They left the city, traveling inland toward the Bekaa Valley. As the Lebanese countryside whizzed by, O'Hara pulled his phone from his pocket and called Dina, to let her know he was safe and that they were on their way to Zahle. He then searched his pockets until he came upon the business card Prince Ahmed had given him. He dialed the number. The phone rang and went to voicemail. O'Hara hung up the phone and cursed.

A moment later the phone rang, showing a blocked number on the screen.

"Yes," he answered.

The familiar voice said something in Arabic, which ended with the hanging intonation of a question.

"Prince Ahmed?" he asked.

"Who is this?" the man asked in English.

"Amjad's American friend."

"I am watching the news," Prince Ahmed said. "Are you okay?"

"I'm fine..." O'Hara hesitated. "What are my chances at taking the Crown Prince up on his offer to visit The Kingdom?"

Omar glanced over with a confused expression.

"Of course, my dear. Can you find your own way here?"

"That's the problem."

"I do not believe we can come to Lebanon, with what has just occurred."

"I see," O'Hara said.

"Can I reach you on this number I just called?" the prince asked.

"It's my mobile. Yes."

"I will call you shortly."

"Okay," O'Hara said. He hung up the phone.

Omar was about to say something, when he was interrupted by the phone ringing, again.

"Yes?" O'Hara said into the phone.

"Can you make it to Jordan? I can have a private jet meet you there."

He looked at Omar, and covered the mouthpiece of his phone with his hand. "Can you get us to Jordan?" he whispered.

Omar shot him a suspicious look, then nodded. "We will need a car that isn't stolen."

"We can take Dina's," O'Hara said.

"I can get you across the Golan, into Jordan," Omar said.

"I can make it to Jordan," O'Hara said into the phone.

"Very well," Prince Ahmed said. "You will make your way to Amman and call me."

"Thank you for this," O'Hara said.

"It is important in our culture to honor our word."

"I will call you from Jordan."

"Yes," the Prince replied. "*Salaam.*"

O'Hara disconnected the line and slipped it back into his pocket. He glanced over at Omar, who shot him a quizzical stare, before turning his attention back to the road.

* * *

It was a tearful reunion. O'Hara and Dina packed a bag and rode with Omar toward the Golan Heights in her Nissan. Somewhere near the border they drove to a checkpoint guarded by four bearded men. They were dressed in olive-green fatigues and armed with assault rifles.

"Hezbollah," Omar said out of the side of his mouth, as he rolled the window down.

A soldier approached and asked something in Arabic. Omar answered, saying a man's name as he pulled a wad of cash from his pocket and stuck it out the window. The soldier accepted the money and studied him for a moment, then angled his head in order to look deeper into the vehicle. He narrowed his eyes at where O'Hara and Dina sat. Over his shoulder he called out to the other three soldiers, who began walking toward them.

The soldier said something to Omar, who turned to O'Hara and Dina. "They want us to get out while they contact a Hezbollah officer that I told them I know."

They all stepped out and stood before two of the soldiers, as the remaining two searched the interior of the vehicle. As the original soldier questioned Omar, the one beside him made a call on a cell phone. Dina began translating under her breath to O'Hara.

"Omar told them we are returning to Jordan and have lost our identification. He asks if the cash he paid was enough to let us pass. He promises that he knows the man whose name he mentioned. The soldier is now trying to call. They also questioned him about the explosion in Beirut, and seem to believe the Jews are responsible. They are telling Omar that they must confirm we are not foreigners, or worse, Jews."

Finding nothing of interest in their search of the vehicle, the two soldiers approached O'Hara and Dina from behind and frisked them. The soldier with the phone finally got hold of someone on the other end of the line and began speaking in rapid Arabic. Dina protested at being groped, until Omar clucked his tongue, indicating she remain silent. The man who was searching O'Hara came upon the Glock at the small of his back and removed it, then shouted something to the others who stopped and looked over.

The same soldier stuck his hand in O'Hara's pockets, first removing cash, and then the Donovan Burke passport. "*Amriki*," he yelled.

A cacophony of shouting ensued and, before O'Hara's mind could process the chaos, Omar drew his pistol and fired three deafening shots into three of the soldiers' heads.

As the remaining soldier raised his rifle to shoot Omar from behind, O'Hara tackled him. Bone-rattling automatic gunfire sprayed as they fell together. Clouds of dirt kicked up into the air as rounds hit the earth. O'Hara pinned the man with the rifle against his chest and began head-butting his face. He felt the man's nose break and sensed the warm wetness of blood against his forehead. A hand suddenly gripped his collar and yanked him backwards.

He looked up to find Omar down on one knee next to the soldier, with his pant leg torn at the thigh and covered in blood. The Israeli pressed his pistol to the Hezbollah soldier's head and pulled the trigger.

"*Yalla*," Omar shouted, and motioned for everyone to get back in the Nissan. He tried to stand before collapsing back to the ground. "There is Hezbollah all along this stretch," he said through clenched teeth. "They will be here any moment, after hearing the shots."

O'Hara picked up his gun from beside a dead soldier and tucked it at his waist. He then crouched down and lifted Omar over his shoulder, around to the passenger side of the vehicle, and set him down on the front seat. Omar ripped the belt off from his own waist and winced as he wrapped his thigh above the wound. He tightened it as best he could. Blood leaked profusely onto his pants. With Dina in the back seat, O'Hara climbed into the driver's seat and sped off toward the Golan Heights. "Hang in there, buddy," he said to Omar.

A few hundred yards across the border they approached a sand-swept Israeli military checkpoint where soldiers were standing with Micro Taver assault rifles aimed at them. Omar motioned for O'Hara to stop the vehicle and wiped his bloody palms on his pants. He leaned his head out the window, holding up two empty hands while shouting in Hebrew. A soldier ordered O'Hara and Dina to exit the vehicle while two others watched Omar struggle out. When they saw his injury they carried him to a holding barracks and laid him on a cot. A field medic was brought in to assess his leg.

Omar remained stoic despite the agonizing pain he must have felt as the medic cut the rest of his pant leg free and poked and prodded the wound. He spoke to the man in Hebrew as more assistants entered the room. One spiked an IV in Omar's arm while the other applied a tourniquet around his upper thigh.

"This treatment I'm getting," Omar said with effort. "The commanding officer of the base is an old friend."

O'Hara and Dina exchanged knowing looks.

A short while later a heavyset man dressed in olive fatigues and smelling of cigarette smoke entered the barracks. He clasped hands with Omar and kissed his cheek while the medic continued to tend to Omar's leg. A brief conversation in Hebrew followed. Omar explained to O'Hara and Dina that, as a personal favor to him, they could leave the Nissan at the base. Safe passage in a military jeep would get them across the Jordanian border along a known Bedouin smuggling route.

The medic spoke a little English and explained that Omar's leg had been shattered above the knee, but that there were no life-threatening injuries. Omar would be airlifted to a hospital in Haifa for proper treatment.

O'Hara could hear a helicopter starting up somewhere nearby. He leaned his head down close to Omar's. "Thank you for everything," he whispered.

Omar forced a slight smile, which ended with a wince. "The morphine is working." He reached his hand up and patted the side of O'Hara's face. "We will see each other again, my friend."

Two more soldiers entered the barracks wheeling a stretcher.

Omar motioned for O'Hara to bring his head down close to his. "These people know nothing about what we were doing in Beirut. Do not speak of it to anyone." As O'Hara nodded, he said, "My ride is waiting. *Amshy*."

***

Outskirts of Amman, Jordan

They rested on the hotel bed, holding one another in the dark. Dina sat between O'Hara's legs, leaning back against his chest as he rubbed her head.

"I'm sorry about dragging you into this mess," he said.

"Why?"

"You never should have gone through what happened at the border."

She shook her head. "We are safe. We are together. This is all that matters."

"I've been around that kind of thing before. It would have been traumatic for you."

She nodded. "But in the end, those men were Hezbollah. And we were an American, an Israeli, and a woman traveling together. If it didn't end that way for them, it would have ended that way for us."

O'Hara wrapped his arms around her shoulders. "I don't have the words," he said.

"You don't need them," she interrupted.

"You can still fly to France. Be with your parents."

"I will go there in time," she said. She reached a hand up and ran her fingers along his arm. "We will. My journey is with you, now."

"It sure feels that way, doesn't it?"

"Yes."

"Why couldn't I have met you twenty years ago?"

"Because we were destined to meet when we did."

He leaned his head over her shoulder and kissed her cheek.

His phone vibrated. He answered it, and was told by an English-speaking man that he should be waiting outside the hotel in fifteen minutes. He hung up the phone and the two of them climbed out of bed and dressed.

As they were about to leave the hotel room, O'Hara held Dina by the waist. He was about to speak, when she leaned in and kissed him. She pulled her head back and was smiling.

"It's okay," she said. "I want this."

Downstairs, an entourage of three black Land Rovers with tinted windows rolled to a stop. The rear passenger door of the middle vehicle swung open. Inside, a light-skinned man with a clean-shaven face, dressed in Saudi traditional garb, was sitting with one leg crossed over the other. He nodded at O'Hara. "Donovan Burke," he said.

O'Hara nodded.

"Please," the man said, gesturing with an open hand.

O'Hara turned to Dina and motioned for her to approach. They climbed in the back and sat next to the man, who gave an order to the driver in Arabic. The driver repeated the command into a microphone clipped to his collar. The vehicles all began to move.

O'Hara remained silent as the entourage navigated the dusty road until it merged onto a paved highway. O'Hara could see the lit buildings of what he assumed to be downtown Amman in the distance.

"You have made some powerful friends," the clean-shaven Saudi said, breaking a long silence.

O'Hara looked over at him.

"You will be well looked after where we are going," the man added. "They have plans for you, once you have taken some time to relax and recover."

O'Hara reached out and took hold of Dina's hand. She closed her eyes and leaned her head against his shoulder. Strips of beaded lights up ahead shone through the windshield. They were approaching an airfield. O'Hara noticed a large white jet parked on the tarmac in the distance, beyond barbed-wire perimeter fencing.

"They have plans for me," he said softly to Dina, and grinned. "Man plans and God laughs."

She forced a tired smile.

He closed his eyes and said a silent prayer of gratitude for having survived Lebanon. For Dina. For Omar. He had yet to digest the truth of how much had been lost in the blast. From one moment in time to the next, all those lives erased. God blinked, he thought.

He sent love to Red, finding small comfort in knowing his best friend was now in the company of his grandmother. Their grandmother. He asked whatever higher power existed to take care of the two of them in whatever followed life as he knew it.

He wondered what Riyadh would be like, and tried to remember waking up that final morning in prison not long ago, unaware of how drastically things were about to change. Could he have ever imagined where his life would end up taking him? Not likely. Things were about to change again, and the thought excited him. He didn't need to know what lay ahead. The only thing he needed was sitting beside him with her hand in his.

ACKNOWLEDGEMENTS

LEBANON RED couldn't have been written without the love and support of my wife Georgie and my daughters Scarlett, Savanna and Stella. I'd like to also thank the following people who made great contributions to the novel: my editor, Elaine Ash, Ferd Beck, Colin Broderick, David Colon, my parents Tom and Lisa McCaffrey, my sister Jackie, my brother Mark, aunts Veronica McCaffrey & b. Frank, Haxhi Rugova, Bryan Rhodes, Maulin Shah, James Poit, Nigel and Sarah Moss, and an especially big thanks to everyone at Black Rose Writing.

NOTE FROM THE AUTHOR

Word-of-mouth is crucial for any author to succeed. If you enjoyed *Lebanon Red*, please leave a review online—anywhere you are able. Even if it's just a sentence or two. It would make all the difference and would be very much appreciated.

Thanks!
Luke McCaffrey

We hope you enjoyed reading this title from:

BLACK ROSE
writing™

www.blackrosewriting.com

Subscribe to our mailing list – *The Rosevine* – and receive **FREE** books, daily deals, and stay current with news about upcoming releases and our hottest authors. Scan the QR code below to sign up.

Already a subscriber? Please accept a sincere thank you for being a fan of Black Rose Writing authors.

View other Black Rose Writing titles at www.blackrosewriting.com/books and use promo code **PRINT** to receive a **20% discount** when purchasing.

CPSIA information can be obtained
at www.ICGtesting.com
Printed in the USA
BVHW080952010822
643527BV00015B/446